'Everyone's unhappy.'

'Rubbish.'

'Yes, they are. Even if they don't parade their sorrows, they have them. People are full of anxiety; they don't know what hangs over them. It's not just the bomb – it's that life is so broken up and pointless. No one believes in anything, yet they want to believe. Oh, I don't know what it is, but it's the same for everyone. Your trouble is you're out of date. You want to be some sort of romantic hero lifted by your sufferings and your sensitive soul above the common run. Well, that's all over now. You've got to stop going round looking for a free gift of perfect love, and try and understand how other people feel.'

He had listened to all this very patiently in order to show her how mistaken she was. He answered seriously: 'Whatever you say, individual relationships are the most important thing in life.'

'I don't deny it. But they're not given you on a plate. You have to earn them. It's no good thinking that every pretty boy you see is going to be the great love of your life. It's jolly unlikely, apart from anything else.'

Also by Olivia Manning
and available from
Mandarin Paperbacks

The Balkan Trilogy
The Rain Forest
School for Love
The Doves of Venus

OLIVIA MANNING

A Romantic Hero

Mandarin

A Mandarin Paperback
A ROMANTIC HERO

First published in Great Britain 1967
by William Heinemann Ltd
This edition published 1992
by Mandarin Paperbacks
Michelin House, 81 Fulham Road, London SW3 6RB

Mandarin is an imprint of the Octopus Publishing Group,
a division of Reed International Books Limited

Copyright © Olivia Manning 1967

Several of these stories have appeared
in magazines and collections.
Acknowledgements are due to *Winter's Tales*,
Voices, the *Kenyon Review*, *Harper's Bazaar*,
Vogue, *Queen*, *Encounter*, *The Saturday Book*
and *The Compleat Imbiber*. The first eight
stories are reprinted from *Growing Up* (1948).

A CIP catalogue record for this title
is available from the British Library

ISBN 0 7493 1199 1

Printed and bound in Great Britain
by Cox & Wyman Ltd, Reading, Berks

This book is sold subject to the condition
that it shall not, by way of trade or otherwise,
be lent, resold, hired out, or otherwise circulated
without the publisher's prior consent in any form
of binding or cover other than that in which
it is published and without a similar condition
including this condition being imposed
on the subsequent purchaser.

The Children

The Children

_____

The pebbles on the beach were shaped like gulls' eggs. Most of them were white. Those that were chipped showed the inner flint like dark glass.

'Where do they all come from?' asked Joseph. 'All shaped the same and grey inside and white outside?'

'Perhaps they're eggs,' said Van. 'Fishes' eggs.'

'Of course they're not. They're stones. Eggs break if you drop them.'

'Perhaps they're frozen – or perhaps they're petrified. Perhaps. Water petrifies things. I read it in a book. And these come out of the water.'

'Then why are they black inside?'

'Things go black inside when they're old.'

Joseph sat on his heels and stared at the flint in his hand. His eyes squinted a little as his brows met in a reflective frown.

Among the stones were pieces of cork, scraps of torn nets and the black tangle of dried weed. Near the sea the weed, still wet, was olive-green. It was pliable and full of air-bladders. Van picked up a large piece and started bursting the bladders one by one. The grey sea, reflecting the grey sky, curled in round her feet.

Joseph let the flint drop and jumped up: 'Come on, let's run to the rocks!'

'I can't. I've got to burst all of them.' Both children stood silent in concentrated attention while one after the other the air-bladders exploded with a squelching sound beneath Van's fingers. After she broke the last one, she swung her arm round in an arc and sent the seaweed flying out over the water. Before it landed she leapt away, calling: 'Come on, then.'

Joseph did not catch her up until they reached the rocks that rose like a difficult stairway to the wall surrounding the garden of their home. They made a detour to visit the largest of the pools that lay in a coign facing the sea. It had to be visited every day because there was no knowing what a tide might leave behind or take away. It lay tranquilly reflecting the sky's silver until they reached it and stood above it, then they could look down on it and see, through the clear, smooth water, the film of fawn-coloured, speckled sand at the bottom. All over the sides the delicate anemones were pearl-pink and flamingo pink. Beside them grew little blood-dark, unvarying jellies.

'Congo's gone,' announced Joseph with a decision that sounded like triumph.

'No, he hasn't,' said Van with equal decision. 'He wouldn't go. He's too lazy. He's under the seaweed.' She poked at a large clump of purple weed that grew like a fan from one side of the pool, but roused only a cloud of sand.

'He's gone, he's gone,' sang Joseph.

Determinedly, Vanessa put her hand behind the weed and forced a large crab to come out into the open. Almost at once it tried to bury itself in the shallow sand.

'Oh no, you don't, Mr Congo,' said Joseph, lifting it by the rim of its shell and placing it on a ledge from which there was no escape. It sidled one way and another, seeking shelter until, finding none, it crouched, with an exposed look, in the open.

[4]

'Do you think he's getting to know us?' asked Van.

'Yes, of course; that's why he stays. He doesn't want to leave us because we're good to him. What shall we feed him on today?'

'I read yesterday that crabs like dead bodies. They eat the eyes first.'

'Do you mean dead people?'

'Yes, drowned people.'

Joseph, who had been getting his penknife out to cut a mollusc from the rock, paused and stared at the crab with disgust.

'It's not his fault,' said Vanessa. 'He doesn't know any better.'

'You mean, if I got drowned he'd eat me – and I've been going to all this trouble to feed him?'

'No, he probably wouldn't eat you. He'd probably save you like the lion with a thorn in its paw.' Vanessa broke off to listen and Joseph, seeing the lift of her head listened too. They could hear their mother calling from the other side of the garden wall. When they caught the tone of her voice, they exchanged a look but did not move.

Joseph whispered: 'I suppose we'd better go.' Van nodded. She put Congo back into the pool before following her brother up the rocks. They knew the path so well they could have climbed it blindfolded. They skirted the edges of the weed-filled crevices and, by a sort of swift balancing on nothing, scrambled up the sheer, slippery rock faces before they had time to fall back again to the ledge below. The climb had become with practice a series of swift, perfected movements that got them in a few minutes to the dry, scaly rock at the top. There, clutching the tufts of hard grass, they could look down into the crevices where they believed the strong-smelling weed hid giant octopi and other secret, colourless monsters.

They came to the leap.

Mrs Clandavy, on the other side of the wall, started calling them again.

'We're coming,' Joseph answered as he took the leap without pausing to measure it or glance down. He went over with his bone-thin legs bent. His knickers, his ragged jersey and his socks were all too short, and his limbs stuck out from them like sticks. His neck, like a thin stalk, held precariously the weight of his large head with its thick, untidy, fawn-coloured hair. Van, a year older, taller and even thinner, followed him easily.

In one place the rock rose to within four feet of the top of the wall. Everywhere else the wall, built of granite during the famine years when labour was cheap, was ten feet high. It had been planned to shut out from the lower windows of the house the view of wild, wind-driven sea that lay between the black rocks and the black, barren, grassless coast of Clare. The romantic generation that followed could not afford to reclaim the view.

Joseph clutched the top of the wall with fingers red as birds' claws. His hair fell forward into his eyes as he swung over and landed softly on the banked-up earth on the other side. Vanessa, following, could hear their mother's voice: 'Why are you children never here when I want you? Why can't you play in your own garden instead of climbing about on the beach? You are getting to look just like the village children. Where is Vanessa?'

Van appeared above the wall, her hair hanging down past her waist and the inverted triangle of her face white above the wilderness of the garden. Because of the high wall the garden was always in shadow. The neglected plants, grown tall and rank, fell about in disorder. Van climbed down the earth bank and disappeared behind a forest of stalks. She parted them and appeared again, waif-thin, her lips and eyes and hair as colourless as her face.

'You look like a tinker's brat,' said Mrs Clandavy, anger and hurt on her face as she stared at the girl.

'Tinkers are dark,' said Van.

'And dirty.'

'I don't look worse than Joseph.'

'He's a boy; it doesn't matter – but you *do* expect a girl to have some pride in her appearance.'

'It's always all right for Joseph and not right for me.' She trailed behind her mother and brother as they went hand-in-hand across the expanse of weed-coarsened lawn towards the open french windows. Joseph turned and grinned at her. She whispered: 'I hate you,' and put her tongue out. He grinned again and did a little dance to show his indifference, but Mrs Clandavy spoilt it by shaking at his hand.

'What's the matter with you, Joseph?' she asked.

Joseph became peevish. 'Why did you call us?'

'There is a man coming from Galway to look at the dining-room table. I don't want to be alone here with him.'

'I knew she didn't really want us,' Van whispered. 'She can't leave us alone a minute.' Then, as Joseph pretended not to hear, she added aloud: 'We haven't fed Congo yet.'

'Oh,' Joseph hung back and wailed. 'We haven't fed Congo. Congo will starve to death.'

'Who is Congo?' their mother asked impatiently.

'Our crab. We feed him every day. We were just going to feed him when you called us.'

'You think more of a crab than you do of your own mother. You never give me a thought here all day by myself while your father's out gallivanting with that woman.

Ungrateful children! It's for your sake that I bear with this life. If you had any love for your mother you would put her before everything. I had no mother or—' Mrs Clandavy shook off Joseph's hand and hurried through the glass door into the drawing-room. She sank into a Louis Quinze chair covered with worn yellow brocade and searched for her handkerchief. Joseph at once threw himself upon her crying: 'Mummy, Mummy, Mummy!' She held him off with one hand while she found the handkerchief tucked in her waistband and then gave a preliminary sniff. Van stood for some moments with a hardened, miserable look before collapsing down at her mother's side and bursting into tears.

'Go away. Go away, both of you. I want none of you. I've always had to bear my troubles alone. All my life I've had to do it, and I can do it now.'

'Oh, Mummy! Oh, Mummy!' sobbed Vanessa and Joseph together. 'You know we love you.'

'Darling Mummy!' Joseph put his arms round her neck and kissed her face until she clutched him and tears came into her eyes.

'At least I have my little boy,' she said.

'And me, too,' howled Van. 'Oh, Mummy, you don't love me at all.'

'Of course I love you.' Mrs Clandavy sat upright and pushed the children off her. 'I love both of you the same. Do get up, Vanessa, and see if you can't do something to help Dorothy in the kitchen. You're getting a big girl, and yet you want to play all the time like a baby.'

'What about Joseph?' Vanessa got to her feet and started moving slowly across the long, dim room.

'What about Joseph? What about Joseph?' her mother mimicked her. 'Is that all you can say? Do you expect a boy to help in the house. When I was your age I was delighted when the cook let me do any little thing in the kitchen – I thought it was a great game. I would never have expected my brothers to do it. You are an unnatural and ungrateful child! What a disappointment this life is! My daughter that should be a comfort to me . . .' Mrs Clandavy's voice broke and Joseph flung his arms round her again while he made faces at Van over her shoulder. Van turned her back on them and stood rubbing her fingers on the glass tops of the little tables that stood in the middle of the room. On the blue velvet beneath the glass were dark ovals, squares and rounds where treasures had once lain. On the walls were larger squares and ovals where the pictures had hung. One large, cobwebbed patch marked the place where the china-cupboard had stood until a week before. Van wandered out of the door and down the passage to the kitchen.

The kitchen was larger than the drawing-room and darker. It had a red flagged floor and a range, rusting in places, that ran the length of one wall. Dorothy was sitting at the kitchen table by the window, staring intently at the palms of her hands. An open book lay beside her. That, Van knew, was the palmistry book, because she had looked at it when Dorothy went to Galway.

She stood in the doorway and waited so long to be noticed that she was at last forced to say ungraciously: 'Is there anything I can do to help you?'

Dorothy did not look round. 'Help?' she queried. She came from the north, and when she wanted to be expressive her voice rose into a squeak: 'Help, did y'say? Get away out of this. Ye're more nuisance than y're worth.'

Van went at once. Anyway, she had offered. She ran up the staircase and then up three narrower flights to the top floor where a corridor with evenly placed windows ran the length of the back of the house. From the windows it was possible to see out beyond Clare and the islands to the far breakers of the Atlantic. At night, in the darkness, with the wind flinging itself against the house, Vanessa found the corridor terrifying. During the day it had a dreamlike lightness and emptiness. She still found it frightening, but in a different and satisfying way. 'It's because of nothing instead of something,' she said. 'It's because there's room to think.'

There were eight windows along the passage. Going from one to the other, the spectator scarcely noticed the change in the view until at the last window he realized he could now see the Aran Islands. If anyone opened the door at the end of the passage and went into Dorothy's room and looked from the side windows, he could not see Clare at all but, instead, the islands and the headlands of the Galway coast. On summer evenings the passage and the bedroom would be full of red sunlight and, with the sea and wind motionless, the silence was concentrated in the air. It was usually at this time that Van felt drawn to go up and tiptoe about Dorothy's room. The windows were always shut and the room had a smell of some sort of ointment. There was a pink celluloid hair-tidy, poke-shaped, filled with neat little twists of Dorothy's ginger hair; and a tray with buttons and pins and two American stamps; and a photograph of a girl in a boater hat holding a dog up near her face. As Vanessa moved about, the few pieces of yellow-varnished furniture, touched by the evening light, stood watching, not relaxing a moment until she tiptoed out and shut the door. Outside she took a breath and stood by one of the windows trembling from head to foot.

Joseph would not go near the passage. 'I hate it,' he said.

'But, why?' asked Vanessa.

'Because . . .' he was vague, but once he said: 'It's like church bells.'

'No, it isn't,' said Van. 'It's quite different. Church bells just make you feel sad, but in the passage there's all sorts of imaginations – outside you. Nice ones, except when it begins to get dark.' In the twilight they became menacing. The passage, growing chilly, seemed to shrink as the light changed colour. Even the familiar sea, rolling and unrolling itself out there with the night spreading over it, seemed threatening. In a panic to escape she would stumble down the flights of stairs to the safety of the living-rooms.

Once Mrs Clandavy, meeting her as she came rushing down with eyes starting from a white face, was astonished when Vanessa clung to her trembling and speechless.

'What is the matter with the child?'

Dorothy, who was following her mistress, said with indifference: 'Och, she's been up in the attic frightening herself again.'

'Is that all!' Mrs Clandavy shook Vanessa off. 'Control yourself, Vanessa, and don't go up to the top floor again if it frightens you. You're always up there.'

'Aye,' agreed Dorothy. 'And poking her wee, sharp nose into my belongings, too.'

'Be quiet, Dorothy.'

'I'll be quiet when it suits me, mem,' and that had started one of the usual quarrels between the two women, with Mrs Clandavy ordering Dorothy to pack her bags and leave the house at once, and Dorothy saying she would not go until she was paid the month's salary owing to her and given her train fare back to Belfast as arranged. Those quarrels were so frequent the children scarcely noticed them. It was the fear of those between their parents that lurked like an evil about the house to spring on them even in the middle of the night.

As Vanessa stood now looking from one of the middle

windows, she could see her mother and Joseph walking hand-in-hand across the lawn. Mrs Clandavy was wearing one of her 'going away' suits that she had had for ten years. She still dressed her hair as on the day she left her home in Edinburgh to become mistress of the Clandavy estate. The children saw their mother's appearance as usual for a lady while the changed fashions of the women in Galway were, they supposed, for people like Dorothy. Watching her mother, Vanessa felt uneasy at being safely up here when she should, she supposed, be down in the garden. Up here she was always liable to feel self-reproach as though secretly, unknown to herself, some part of her were on the side of those who made her mother unhappy. Sometimes she would be so stricken with guilt, that she would become angry with her mother and think: 'Why must she always make us miserable?' and then she would remember her tall, beautiful, proud mother crumpled and crying in a chair, and her anger would collapse inside her. If her mother let her comfort her, Van would have felt strong and successful and brave. She would have been a strong protector against unhappiness – but, instead, her comfort always failed. Mrs Clandavy always became impatient with her and shook her off so instead of being a strong protector, she was only an impotent, unhappy child.

When Van tried to speak of this to Joseph, he did not know what she was talking about. His mother called him her baby, her little boy; there was a bond between them that gave him security and if he were irritated, it was because his mother demanded more than he was prepared to give.

'She doesn't really want me down there,' thought Vanessa and yet she was not sure and not consoled.

Dorothy appeared from the house with a little fat man in a

black suit and bowler hat. As Mrs Clandavy looked down on him from her unusual height, he snatched off the hat and bowed. She said something and, still holding to Joseph, led the way back to the house.

Van knew there was not much fun to be got out of the furniture dealer. Mrs Clandavy thought she had a good business head, but the dealer seemed to have a better one. He always told them how the Troubles had changed the value of everything. Even the fine houses that skirted Galway Bay stood empty, 'To Let or For Sale' posted up before each and no one willing to give half a crown for the lot of them. As for antique furniture! Who would be wanting it at such a time? There was never an American seen in Galway these days. Trade had gone from the town and half the shops were shut down. The gentry – saving one or two like herself – had taken themselves off long ago.

Ten minutes later Joseph called to Van from the stairs. When she did not answer, he tiptoed to the passage entrance and saw her leaning against one of the window-panes with her forehead pressed to the glass and her eyes shut. When he whispered her name, she opened her eyes and turned in a sleepy way.

'What were you thinking about?' he whispered.

She shook her head. 'I wasn't thinking.'

'What were you doing?'

'Trying to get out. When I was young I used to be able to get right outside myself and see myself separate, but now I can't do it any more. I can't get out. Can you?'

'I don't know. I've never tried. Let's go downstairs.'

'Come and look out of the window.'

'No. Let's go and feed Congo,' he began running down the stairs and she followed him. The second landing was dark and when they reached it, she suddenly started crying. She leant against the wall and sobbed. Joseph turned on the stairs and looked at her. 'What's the matter?'

'Mummy doesn't love me. No one loves me.'

'Oh, come on,' Joseph turned and went on down the stairs. Vanessa wiped her nose with the back of her hand and repeated urgently: 'Poor Congo, poor Congo!' Before they could get out of the house Dorothy called them to their tea which she laid now in the kitchen to save the climb up two flights to the nursery. They ate their thick slices of bread and margarine quickly before hurrying out of the kitchen door and down the garden.

Mrs Clandavy had been watching for them. She was sitting by the open drawing-room door. When they appeared, she put down her teacup and called to them. They did not go to her, but paused and shouted back: 'We're going to feed Congo.'

'You've had enough play for one day. Come here.'

'But we haven't fed Congo,' Joseph did not move and his voice grew peevish. 'He'll starve to death.'

'Please, Joseph, do not argue with me. It is not very often that I see either of you. What life is there here for me? What happiness? I have nothing now but you two children. He went out early this morning and hasn't been back all day. I have no one. I am all alone. Even my children, for whom I have sacrificed everything, desert me.'

Joseph and Van exchanged glances that were resentful and guilty. They moved slowly towards the drawing-room door. After a moment Van stopped. 'You go,' she said, 'I'll feed Congo. She doesn't want me. She'd rather have you.'

'Why should you go and feed him and leave me to—'

Mrs Clandavy's voice from the doorway interrupted sternly: 'I hear you, my boy. So that's all you think of your poor mother!'

[14]

Joseph looked at her, silenced, then burst out: 'I don't care. I don't care.'

'God!' wailed Mrs Clandavy. 'What have I done to be cursed with such children?'

'Oh, not me,' Vanessa had turned pale. 'Not me, Mummy, darling. I love you.' She ran and dropping to her knees, pressed her face into her mother's lap.

Mrs Clandavy clicked her tongue impatiently.

'I love you,' Van insisted as her mother tried to move aside from her.

Joseph, aloof and angry in the doorway, shouted sternly: 'She doesn't love you. She wanted to go off and feed Congo and leave me here.'

'You're both the same. Neither of you cares one iota for me. *Nobody* cares,' Mrs Clandavy had begun feeling for her handkerchief again, when a noise in the hall made her stiffen. She whispered sharply: 'Is that your father?'

But it was only Dorothy come to take the tea-tray away. Mrs Clandavy sat upright in her chair, a strange expression on her face as she stared into the garden. When Dorothy left the room, she began speaking slowly to herself. 'This has been going on for some time. Dorothy has seen them together more than once. I know who she is – the vulgar creature!'

Van and Joseph glanced at each other and turned red. Their mother suddenly stood up. 'I know what we'll do – we'll go and see. We'll go and find him. If he doesn't know when to return to his own home, we'll go and remind him.'

Van left on her knees, jumped up, brightening at the prospect of adventure in a way that annoyed her mother, who said: 'Go and make yourself tidy. Put on your hat and gloves. Where is your other frock?'

'You said Dorothy would wash it. It's in the clothes' basket.'

'Get it out and put it on. It couldn't be dirtier than that one.'

Vanessa's hat and gloves were becoming too small. She had not worn them since the dog-cart had been sold and she and Joseph had stopped going over to have lessons with the O'Neil children. Mrs Clandavy had sent Lady O'Neil a note saying she thought her children would learn more if she taught them herself. After that Van and Joseph had been put into the library to read anything they could find among the remaining books.

Vanessa came down the stairs with her hat on the back of her head.

'Where are your gloves?' Mrs Clandavy was dressed as though for paying calls and carried a taffeta parasol much split at the creases.

'They won't go on.'

'Then you must carry them.'

'But why? What is the good if they won't go on?'

'Don't argue with me, Vanessa. Get your gloves.'

The sun had come out low on the horizon as they walked down the drive between the overhanging trees and tall grasses. Behind them the grey of the long-fronted, eighteenth-century house stood out delicately against the pink sky. The green of grass and leaves was tinged with blue in the shadows. The air, becoming misty, was full of the summer-evening scents. Mrs Clandavy, walking rigidly beneath her rigid sailor hat and scarcely moving her shoulders, restrained the children from running excitedly about.

Joseph, fastened into his too-small sailor suit, was held prisoner by her hand. Van, walking beside the elegantly-pecking parasol, felt burdened by her kid gloves. She wanted to throw them away. She changed them from one hand to the other as they grew more hot and sticky. Then she thought of tying them to her belt and, until her mother noticed them and made her carry them again, she danced ahead with relief.

They passed the derelict stone lodge and out through the gates to the road. Mrs Clandavy, afraid of being seen walking by the villagers, hurried them across the road to the lane opposite. There they were hidden again in a rich shade of trees. Joseph and Vanessa kept watching the strange tenseness of their mother's attitude as she walked between them, but they avoided each other's eyes. They walked a long way up the slope of the nearest hill. A chilly twilight darkened the trees. The children began to tire and their interest to flag, but their mother remained conscious only of her own intention. She began now to walk with her head thrust forward a little, her cheeks flushed while an odd, glinting look held her face in unnatural hardness. When Joseph trailed behind and pulled at her hand, she took no notice.

'I'm tired,' he whimpered.

Van, frightened by her mother's strangeness and the strangeness of the late evening, said: 'Let's go back, Mummy.'

'We haven't fed Congo yet,' said Joseph.

'Be quiet,' whispered their mother sharply. 'Be quiet, both of you.'

They were surprised into silence, growing curious and excited again as Mrs Clandavy paused and stared down at a small house in a hollow fifty yards below.

'An English lady lives there,' whispered Van. 'She paints pictures. She let us look at them once.'

'I know. Be quiet and stay there.' Mrs Clandavy, bending slightly, made her way round the rim of the hollow. Above her the hill rose darkly against the darkening blue of the sky. A few stars winked out. The house below, all its windows black, looked deserted. As the children watched, the figure of

[17]

their mother seemed to waver and become lost in the uncertain twilight. Van and Joseph, suddenly terrified, rushed after her and seized her and crouched into her skirt. With a last penetrating stare down into the hollow, she swung round and started back home again. The children would not leave go of her skirts until she slapped at their hands and ordered them to walk with dignity. They had to trot to keep up with her.

'Perhaps the lady has gone away,' said Van breathlessly.

'Not she. They're off together somewhere.'

'Who?' asked Joseph. 'Do you mean Daddy?'

'Be quiet. How dare you ask me such a question!'

They returned in silence to the dark drive and the dark house.

Van was on her way up to the passage next morning when she heard her father return. She leant over the banister and saw him wander into the hall. Like the children, he was fair and very thin. His face from a distance looked boyish, but closer was lined and hollow. Van was careful to keep hidden and she watched him, a mysterious creature, with wonder.

His wife had been listening for him. She came into the hall and fixed him with her eyes while he turned slowly to look at her. When he saw her, he hurried towards the library door. Her voice pounced on him.

'Where have you been?'

He seemed jerked to a sudden and angry sharpness. 'Leave me alone,' he shouted, 'damn you, leave me alone.' He flung himself into the library and tried to slam the door in her face. Before it closed, she held it and wedged her foot in it. They pushed the door, one on either side of it, in silence. Van, watching, could hear her mother panting with the effort. She tried to run safely out of sight and hearing, but Mrs Clandavy, seeing something move above, cried: 'Vanessa, come and help me.'

Van paused unwillingly, then began very slowly to descend. Suddenly she started to run. She hurled herself down against the door, beating at it with all her might and whispering: 'My poor Mummy, my poor Mummy!'

Almost at once Denis Clandavy let go his hold on the door and Van and her mother fell forward as it opened. He stood in the middle of the room looking sullenly away from them. Mrs Clandavy was flushed and shaken, but she regained herself quickly and repeated implacably: 'Where have you been?'

He glanced over his shoulder and said: 'Go away, Vanessa.'

As she moved to go, her mother put an arm round her shoulder and held her. 'Stay, Vanessa.' Vanessa stood looking first at one of her parents, then at the other. In spite of herself she was hurt and touched by her father's drooping solitary figure as he stood there in the wrong. She wished she could show him she was not entirely against him, but she could not be disloyal to her mother, her wronged and suffering mother whom she adored so that her eyes now filled with tears.

Denis Clandavy moved slowly over to the window and stood between the heavy, dusty curtains, pressing his forehead against the glass. Vanessa thought she knew exactly how he felt as he stood there. She wriggled in an embarrassed way and whispered:

'Joseph will be looking for me.'

Mrs Clandavy pushed her angrily away. 'Then go and find him. Go, at once, I've always had to fight my battles alone.' Her voice broke. 'No one cares anything for me,' she said.

As Vanessa stood wretchedly, her mother pushed her out of the room and closed the door. She waited outside for some moments until an uproar of voices broke out in the room, then she made off to the garden. Joseph was standing just inside the drawing-room.

'Another row?' he asked with morose resignation.

She nodded. They were not really on speaking terms. Congo had gone with the last tide and each had blamed the other. They were now waiting until there could be some excuse for a reconciliation.

Suddenly Joseph came hopping out of the room on one foot and toppled over and called out: 'Oh!' very loudly. Vanessa looked sideways at him and stuck out her lower lip. When Joseph caught her eye he began to turn somersaults. 'Bet you can't do this,' he said.

'Bet I can.'

'Go on, then, do it.' They turned somersaults until the reconciliation was effected, then they sat up. Joseph said: 'Let's go and look for frogs.' They went out of the garden by a side gate to avoid overhearing the accusations now filling the house, and walked along the shore road. The moorland grass was very long and filmy with damp. A mist hid all the hills and islands. There was nothing to be seen but an immediate circle of bright grass and stones and the shore.

Joseph said: 'It will probably go on all day now.'

'Yes, and Dorothy will go off to Galway and we'll get no tea.'

'We'd better eat some blackberries.'

To the children it seemed that these quarrels filled the house like a furious wind that ignored yet overwhelmed them. They found it safer to keep out of sight of their mother who would, if she saw them, call them in to support her and not let them escape again. They had got into a habit of listening at doorways before entering and, if they heard a quarrel, keeping away from it. Sometimes they found some bread in the kitchen which they took down to eat on the shore.

'One day I'll run away,' said Joseph.

'And leave Mummy?'

After a thoughtful pause he said: 'I'll take her with me.'

'What about me?'

'You can come if you like.'

'What about him?'

'You don't jolly well think I'd take him, do you? We wouldn't have to go if he weren't here.'

Vanessa did not reply. She turned up into the long grass and began looking for frogs. In a few moments her canvas shoes were soaked. The mist, like a fine rain in the air, brushed over her skin as though it were a veil. The brambles, covered with great, waterlogged berries, trailed over the grass. The children had grown up in this damp atmosphere and were not much affected by it. It was only on rare summer days that the sun broke through to reveal the islands and the mountains that had been there all the time. There would not be many more days like that before the endless rain of winter settled in.

Van called: 'Where are you Joseph?'

'Here, eating blackberries.'

She went over to him and they stood by the long, low bushes eating berries that fell off at a touch. Small-bodied, spindle-legged spiders ran from them as the movement of twigs broke the wet, silver webs. Silver globes of dew rolled from the bramble leaves.

A small boy, trailing a stick after him, appeared out of the mist and stared at them. Half a dozen others appeared behind him. He pointed at the Clandavys and asked his friends in awe: 'Is it eating them they are?'

Joseph stared back at the boys and solemnly put out his blackened tongue. Then he threw a berry into the air, caught it in his mouth and ate it with elaborate enjoyment.

'They're not yours,' he said.

The small boys stared until the Clandavys began to feel uneasy and to realize that whatever the trouble was, it was not a question of ownership. Suddenly the leader shouted: 'The crown of thorns of the Blessed Jesus was made from brambles. Yer damned. You've eaten them. Yer damned. Yer damned.'

Van and Joseph, standing on the ridge of the hillock, stared down, wide-eyed, at the boys. The boys realized they had made an impression.

One at the back whispered: 'They're the Clandavys.'

The leader agreed. 'And everyone knows they're mad,' he said.

That meant nothing to Vanessa and Joseph, they had heard it too often, but no one had warned them about the blackberries. They retreated slowly with their large, pale eyes fixed on the boys. When they felt it was safe to turn, they swung round and ran out of sight. The jeers of the boys followed them. The leader threw his stick after them, but it fell into the bushes. When they had got out of sight they stood and panted.

'You know what the O'Neils said,' said Vanessa. 'They said we were Protestants. Moira said we were damned.'

'I thought it was because we hadn't any money,' said Joseph.

'Moira said we hadn't any money because we were damned. She didn't say we were damned because we hadn't any money.'

'Anyway,' said Joseph sullenly. 'She doesn't know. How could she know – not for sure, anyway.'

'But perhaps it's because we eat blackberries.'

'Well, it's not fair. Why should God put blackberries there if he doesn't want us to eat them?'

'It might be a trap. You know what God's like!'

'Well, I don't believe Jesus would mind – and it was his crown. He's supposed to have done it to save everyone.'

'Yes, but not us. Moira said not us because we're Protestants.'

After a long pause, Joseph said: 'I don't care,' but he was feeling sick. They walked very slowly and heavily up the lower slopes of the hills and out of the mist. In the distance they saw their father walking towards them, his gaze on the ground. They moved silently in a detour to avoid him. He had once stopped and spoken to them, and, although they had not told their mother, she had somehow discovered it and questioned them and accused them of disloyalty for listening to him. As they dodged behind a bush, he looked up and saw them. They stood still, but he only glanced at them as though they were strangers and walked on. The children ran in the other direction for a short distance, then paused and looked after him.

'Do you really think he is wicked?' asked Van.

Joseph frowned, then said defiantly: 'Yes, I do.' He stared angrily at her and she turned red. After they had walked for some minutes, Joseph burst out more defiantly than before: 'He is wicked. He makes Mummy cry.'

'Yes,' Vanessa agreed at once. As she thought of her mother crying, something rose in her throat and she felt as though she were being choked.

'We can go home now,' said Joseph.

When they reached the house they saw the O'Neil coachman in the drive. He had brought a note from Lady O'Neil saying that Charles, Moira and Herbert were longing to see their little friends again. Joseph and Vanessa must come to tea tomorrow and she would send the carriage for them.

Mrs Clandavy was on the point of refusing the invitation

when Van and Joseph ran into the hall. 'You can't go,' she said before they could speak. 'Your clothes are a disgrace and you've only yourselves to blame.'

'But we want to go, we want to go,' cried the children. They stood well in view of the coachman and burst into tears.

'Come into the drawing-room,' Mrs Clandavy commanded them, but they would not move. She glared with exasperation at the coachman whose sympathies were so obviously with the children.

'Do you want to go?' she asked Joseph. 'Do you want to leave your mother alone in the house all afternoon?'

'Yes, I do,' said Joseph.

'Do the O'Neils mean more to you than your own mother?'

'I want to see Moira,' sobbed Vanessa.

'I want to see Herbert's Hornby train,' Joseph shouted.

'Very well,' Mrs Clandavy decided. 'Joseph can go. Vanessa, you stay here with me like a good girl.'

'Oh, no! Oh, no!' Vanessa buried her face in her arms and wept bitterly.

Mrs Clandavy's mouth set in a thin line, then she put her arm round Joseph's shoulders and said: 'Let her go, the crybaby! She's a spoilt, selfish girl. She cares nothing for her poor mother. Joseph is mother's baby, mother's pet lamb. He'll stay here and keep his mother company.'

'But I want to go,' Joseph's voice rose to a furious scream. 'I haven't seen the Hornby train for months.'

The coachman, standing in the porch, moved uncomfortably. Mrs Clandavy said fiercely to the world: 'You devote your life to your children – and this is the thanks you get.' Then she went and wrote a note of acceptance.

Dorothy was persuaded to wash Vanessa's dress and next afternoon Mrs Clandavy helped the children to get ready. She

[24]

had made no more complaints about their going. It was one of those times – becoming rare now – when it seemed she understood how they felt. It was as though she had given them a surprise gift. They became talkative and gay with gratitude. Vanessa, thinking back, believed she could remember a long, long time ago when her mother had always been like this: when they had loved her not because she was unhappy and suffering for their sakes, but because she loved them. Vanessa looked up with inquiry into her mother's eyes and saw them softened and sweet, but almost at that moment they seemed to look inward and grow dark.

'Don't forget that I'm here alone,' she said and they stopped laughing and wanted to get away.

Their gaiety returned as they were carried with beautiful ease over the narrow coast road towards the town that glittered beneath the uncertain sky. The mist had lifted. Over Clare a black cloud-ridge accentuated the whiteness of the clouds bellying up from the east, and the blueness of the sky above them. The little, flipping waves, skirting the road at high tide, a few feet from the carriage wheels, sparkled black and blue against the rust-red of the gravel.

They turned inland before they reached Galway. The children sat stiffly in the elegant carriage. They had not seen the O'Neil children since they had stopped sharing their lessons. The coachman turned in his seat and said to Van and Joseph:

'There's talk that the little mistress and masters will be away to London.'

'Oh?' whispered the Clandavys.

'Sir James is representing his country there – he's a fine man and a good Catholic even though he did marry an Englishwoman, and we're all proud of him this day.' He turned back again and gave a little flick at the horses that set them trotting.

The house could be seen in the distance. The sunlight was brilliant on the road, but within the grounds a shadow fell from the puce-dark clouds mounting rapidly up from Clare. A sudden wind weighted the trees. They bent from their tips and the white undersides of the leaves glimmered like a movement of hands in the gloom. The moss-tender up-sweeping of the lawn was an acid green as though lit by lime-light. In the distance, at the crest of the lawn's rise, the long low house was startlingly embossed against a thunderous sky.

As they approached it, the house disappeared behind trees. The shadow crept upon the carriage; the wind crept over the children and they shivered. The long tails of the grey, delicate-footed horses were swept to one side. When they slowed down at the gates, the pallid light picked out the ridges of the stonework and the two little lions, like Chinese lions, each balanced on the top of a thin pillar.

'Hello, Mrs Galty,' shouted Joseph to the old woman tugging open the gates. She lifted a face that always looked blind and wrinkled as though in a glare of light, and waved, as delighted as they by their return. They had passed before she could say anything. In the leafy gloom of the drive there was complete silence. Van and Joseph had expected Moira and Herbert to be waiting for them on the terrace as they used to do, but there was no one. That chilled the Clandavys a little. The rain started falling in large, splashing drops over the terrace. There was a rumble of thunder.

The door was opened by a new butler who did not even know their names. They said they knew where the nursery was. As they went upstairs, their spirits had fallen and they felt only apprehension. The English Lady O'Neil came trailing her tea-gown across the first landing. As she went past, she turned and saw the children ascending hand-in hand. She smiled without pausing and fluttered her fingers at them. 'You'll find them all up there. Storm coming, so Miss Hedley brought them in. They're looking forward so much to seeing you. So excited!' She drifted away. Van and Joseph felt brighter as they went through the white-painted door that led to the back stairs and the nursery.

Charles, looking enormous, almost another person with his huge hands and knees, sat doubled up in one of the little nursery chairs. He was reading and did not lift his head as they entered. Herbert and Moira were sitting in the window-seat playing draughts. They stared and said: 'Oh, hello!' without interest and went on with their game. Van and Joseph stood by the table and watched. After a moment, Van looked shyly round at Charles. He was biting the side of his thumb as he sat there absorbed by his book. His ears looked very red and prominent and his features seemed to have grown heavier. Van was longing for him to look up and see her, yet terrified of his doing so. He kept his eyes on his book. He was frowning and when he turned a page he turned it very quickly, as though he were reading in a great hurry. Herbert and Moira were quarrelling over their game.

'You can't do that, you silly fool,' said Herbert.

'Yes, I can, you silly fool,' said Moira.

This quarrelling made the Clandavy children feel even more excluded. They stood silently by the table while a flood of rain obscured the windows. The darkness in the room made Vanessa want to cry.

Suddenly Miss Hedley came in. 'Moira, Herbert,' she called in her energetic way. 'Here are your little friends. Have you no welcome for them?'

'We said "Hello",' said Herbert, not pausing in the game or the quarrel. 'It's not your move, you silly fool.'

'Don't call your sister a silly fool,' said Miss Hedley. 'And let Van and Joseph play, too.'

'Four people can't play draughts.'

Miss Hedley was looking for something in a cupboard as she talked: 'Then play something else.'

'We can't,' said Moira. 'We haven't finished this game.'

Miss Hedley found what she wanted and bustled out again. Van and Joseph went on standing by the table. They stared blankly at the draughts board which they had not seen before. The game seemed to go on for a long time, but it was finished at last. Moira sighed as she dropped the pieces, one by one, loudly into a box. Herbert turned and in a patronizing tone asked Joseph: 'What would you like to play?'

'Can't we play trains?'

'Oh, lord!' Herbert yawned. 'Those old trains!' He did not move from the seat, but sat with his feet under him, opening and shutting the draughts board. Joseph was bewildered and silenced. Six months before the trains had been their chief interest.

Herbert had had his black curls cut off and looked much older. Moira, very dark, pink-cheeked and blue-eyed, sat on the edge of the seat and tapped her toes on the floor as though she did not know what to say. At last Vanessa, asking what she had been dying to ask, heard her own voice coming out high, affected and unreal: 'Are you really going to London?'

'I don't know. Daddy doesn't want us to go.'

'Yes, we are going,' said Herbert. 'Mummy wants us to go and we always do what Mummy wants.'

'No, we don't always.'

'Yes, we do, you silly fool!'

'No, we don't, you silly fool!'

The new quarrel went on like an unenthusiastic tennis set until a maid came in with a tray and started setting the table.

Things improved as they ate tea. Joseph managed to be drawn into an argument between Moira and Herbert about the size of London.

'It's bigger than Galway,' said Moira.

'No it's not, you silly fool,' said Herbert.

'It is,' Joseph shouted without thinking. 'It's bigger than Dublin.'

'You silly fool, it's not.'

'You silly fool, it is,' Joseph flushed at finding himself back in the midst of things and his spirit returned. 'It's twice as big as Dublin and the river's twice as wide and there are millions of people.'

'Millions!' Herbert was scornful. 'Millions! Listen to that!'

Charles, absorbed by his own thoughts, sat folding slices of bread, butter and jam into his mouth. He was home from his first term at a public school. His large round, shiny knees appeared above the top of the nursery table.

'Charles,' Moira called to him as though he were a long way away. 'Isn't London bigger than Dublin?'

'What?' asked Charles in a strange, deep voice. Vanessa looked up, startled by it and blushing, but Moira seemed used to it. 'Isn't London bigger than Dublin?' she persisted.

'Yes,' Charles said and returned to his own thoughts.

After Joseph had been proved right he found it easier to claim attention. He told an elaborate story about the intelligence of the lost Congo. Then Moira said to Vanessa: 'Uncle Samuel found that old photograph.'

'The figurehead?'

'Yes, the one with the telescope.'

'Oh, Moira, can we go and see it.'

'Yes, of course.'

The storm had passed. Crystalline, water-jewelled sunlight

sparkled over the grass outside. The clouds were sinking out of sight behind the prune-purple masses of the woods beyond the lawn.

Herbert and Joseph went off to see the ferrets.

The lawn behind the house ran down to a lake with two swans. Moira and Vanessa walked arm-in-arm to the lake's edge. The swans came drifting towards them as though blown by a wind. They eyed the girls with little, cold eyes, missing nothing, yet with a show of the greatest indifference. Moira had the bread and butter left over from tea. She stood at the edge of the lake breaking the slices with slow deliberation.

'Is Castor as bad as ever?' asked Van.

'Worse, if anything,' said Moira. 'Just watch.' She threw a piece of bread into the water. With business-like agility but no loss of dignity, one of the swans jabbed down his neck and devoured it. Then he righted his head again and moved it with self-possessed awareness on the long, unmoving curve of his neck. Moira threw the next piece away from him towards the other swan, Pollux, but Castor had swallowed it before his brother could see where it had fallen. Two slices went that way while poor Pollux, trapped behind Castor's movements as behind a barrier, sailed backwards and forwards in hurt and perplexed agitation.

'He's a beast,' said Moira. 'Go away, Castor, you beast, you pig! Here, Pollux!' Pollux tried to come but was edged back by Castor. 'Pollux, Pollux, this is for Pollux!' Moira flung the bread over Castor's head and it fell neatly at the swell of Pollux's breast. 'Now, Pollux, you idiot!' But Castor dodged back and the bread disappeared.

'This is disgusting. We'll give him no more.' Moira took Vanessa's arm and marched away. The swans followed, waddling up on to the grass and making harsh noises.

'Oh, here you are!' She flung the rest of the bread far out into the lake and marched off, leaving them to swim for it. 'I bet that pig Castor woolfs the lot,' she said.

The shadow of the clouds retreating before them, the girls passed into the woods that separated the house from the dower-house which was let to Moira's great-uncle, a retired admiral.

Moira, holding Vanessa's arm as affectionately as she had ever done, talked about London. If they did go – and she now seemed very much more hopeful about it – their mother had promised they would be invited to lots of parties.

'Especially at Christmas,' said Moira. 'And I shall have lots of new dresses.'

Last Christmas the Clandavy children had spent the day with the O'Neils, but they had paid for it afterwards because Mrs Clandavy had spent the day alone. Vanessa thought of Christmas coming again.

'You're very quiet,' said Moira.

'Christmas will be awful here if you go,' said Vanessa.

'Um,' agreed Moira vaguely. She was thinking that Vanessa had grown dull. There had been a time when their companionship had been a perpetual joy that had heightened the intelligence and imagination of both. Now Moira felt as though she were having to deal charitably with one of the poor or outcast.

'Why didn't you come and see us before?' she asked.

'We haven't got the dog-cart now.'

'Mother would have sent the carriage. She wrote and told your mother she would send it any time.'

'I didn't know.'

'Well, you could come again – but, of course, we're going to London.' It seemed quite definite now. The two girls became silent. Moira felt this friendship was finished – she had felt it from the first moment when Joseph and Vanessa had entered the nursery like strangers and instead of demanding attention, had stood there with that silly look on their faces. She did not mind very much, she had too many other things with which to occupy herself.

Van thought with wonder of the time when she and Joseph, more inventive than the O'Neils, had been dominant here. Now, feeling keenly her separation from the comfort and tranquillity of this place, she could not think of anything to say.

'Can you see the queen?' asked Moira.

'Yes. Has she been newly painted?'

'Yes. Uncle Samuel did it, but we helped. It was great fun.'

When they came out of the woods on to the dower lawn, there the two figureheads stood in the down-creeping, pollen colour of the evening light. On the right was the queen – a fine, upstanding woman, ten feet tall, in an ermine-edged corslet of scarlet above sweeping royal-blue skirts. She had brilliantly reddened lips curling thickly in a fixed smile, and a red spot on each cheek. Her eyes were egg-shaped, the pupils black and there were black curls beneath her gilded crown. She would have looked brazen had it not been for the regalia. As it was, she held the sceptre and orb as one born to rule and seemed always about to rise out of the waves, never down, always up and up to some ever-rising wave-crest. The bright folds of her skirts seemed to be dragging, taut and heavy, out of the sea of grass. Vanessa found it slightly dizzying to watch her: she was never still, never just there, but always quivering on the point of ascent so the eye rising to follow her was surprised to find she had not moved.

The queen, of course, had been in the Royal Navy. The other figurehead had come from a merchant ship called *The Laughing Sailor*. The whole of the sailor's red-and-white face, beneath the round black hat, was caught up in a grin like the face of a ventriloquist's doll. He had one arm across his middle, where his blue vest met his white trousers, and the other arm was behind his back. But, although his upper half was dancing the hornpipe, his legs disappeared into the cutwater and were imprisoned there. Once the waves had kept him in unceasing motion, but now he was rigid and rather pathetic with his wooden grin and his arms held not as though he were dancing but as though he were bowing out of the wood across to the contemptuous queen.

The girls stood and looked up at the two figures, vivid there in their hobby-horse colours, English and alien against the lavender-gilt evening rises of the Celtic hills.

'Did I tell you,' said Moira, 'that I'm going to school after Christmas.'

'No. Are you really?'

'Yes, to Paris.'

'Goodness! To Paris!'

Van stood with her mouth half open looking quite stupefied. Moira seemed to have passed right out of her world; to have become another, a grown-up person.

'Here's Uncle,' said Moira in a relieved voice. She had been afraid Vanessa was going to cry.

'So you've come back,' said the Admiral, holding out his small plump hands. Short and stout, he came to a standstill expressing delight, his round, red face half hidden in white King Edward VII whiskers and beard. He was still holding his gold-rimmed spectacles in his left hand.

'The figurehead with the telescope,' shouted Van, running straight to him.

'I have it,' he said as he caught her. 'My dear little girl, where have you been all this time?' When she did not reply he did not ask again, for he had heard all the gossip from Lady

O'Neil. He put an arm round Vanessa's shoulder and held out his free hand to Moira. The three walked along the path between the beds of velvet-dark dahlias to the house.

'Where's young Joseph?' he asked.

'Gone to see the ferrets.'

The dower-house had none of the spaciousness of the house. It had been built much later, in Victorian Gothic, and had small, many-cornered, high rooms and narrow windows. To the crowded furniture had been added the museum of the Admiral's possessions: nautical instruments, photographs of ships, objects that had been presented to him in strange ports, things that sailors had made to while away long voyages, and curios from China, Jamaica, Australia and the South Sea Islands. Uncle Samuel had always given the children the run of the dower-house. They were at home there, and Vanessa felt at home again as she entered the front room and smelt its familiar smell of camphor wood.

'Here we are,' he said, taking down a photograph from the crowded mantelpiece. 'That's the figurehead just as it was taken from the ship after they salvaged her: You can see it in the Portsmouth Dockyard Museum now. And there's the signalman's telescope hanging round the neck just as they found it.'

Van plumped down on to the little stool by the fireplace where she used always to sit, and stared at the long, anguished face of the wooden *Eurydice* sinking back into the underworld, never to return again. The long, wooden hands were raised with all the long, round, pointed fingers separate. And there, like a necklace, hung the telescope on a cord round the column of her neck.

'And I found this, too,' said Uncle Samuel. 'It is a photograph of the *Eurydice*'s captain, Maurice Hare. He was one of the finest seamen of his day.'

'Oh!'

Moira knelt beside Vanessa and stared at the two photographs as though she had never seen them before. They peered into the face of the handsome captain who had been drowned so long ago. Vanessa remembered the story that Uncle Samuel had told them when she last saw him, and the ship under all possible sail, flying before the Channel wind on that glittering Sunday afternoon in May. The island cliffs were very near. She saw from behind them the encroach of the black cloud, the change in the light and the whiteness of the ship against the steel-dark waters. Then a sudden uproar of wind and all the air blind with snow; a fury of storm passing as quickly as come; and everyone, in the wet brilliance of the returned sun, asking: 'Where is the ship? Where is the beautiful ship?', and the coastguard on Culver Cliff shouting: 'Where is the *Eurydice*?' and searching the waters through his glass to see only the two little black heads of the seamen, Cuddiford and Fletcher, clinging to their life-belt. Gone was Captain Hare and gone all the young men, the young boys browned by the South Seas' sun, newly come from adventure, who had been watching the approach of the Ventnor cliffs, impatient now they were so nearly home and filled with a hundred stories for the astonishment of their mothers – all gone, leaving the waters smooth, and nothing left but the two stupid seamen who made a fortune touring the fairs of England with their famous life-belt and drank themselves to death.

Van looked up at the little, plump admiral who stood by the fireplace cutting the end off a cheroot. She swallowed and said: 'You promised to tell us about another one.'

'Ah, yes! The *Atalanta*.' The admiral put the cheroot in his mouth and stared out of the window with his faded blue eyes. Then he looked behind him, found his favourite basket-chair and sat down. He lit the cheroot and took it out of his mouth and gazed at it thoughtfully for some moments before putting it back and settling down to smoke it.

'It was in the year 1879,' he began, then paused and gave a deep sigh. The basket-chair creaked as he wriggled into it more comfortably and crossed his short legs. He slipped his heel out of his uppermost slipper and let it dangle from his toes. At last he continued: 'There was a hulk lying in the Portsmouth Dockyard from which the water-police used to watch for smugglers and landing of stores against regulations. The Admiralty decided to roof her over, fit her out as a full-rigged ship with mast and yards, and send her off for a winter cruise with the First Class boys who had passed through the Harbour training-ships. This was all done, and when she arrived at the Bermudas, she moored inside the breakwater at the very spot where the *Eurydice* had moored two years previously.

Van, leaning forward with round eyes, asked: 'And were you there? Did you see her?'

'Yes, I was there on the old *Bellerophon*, the first of the Ironclads. I did my first long commission at the West Indies station. I saw the *Eurydice* come and go, and then the *Atalanta*. She stayed about ten days before making ready for the homeward voyage. A curious thing happened! Very curious! Three sailors and a marine had been sentenced to long terms of imprisonment for serious offences against naval discipline, and they were ordered to be returned home on the *Atalanta*. When they were being marched to the quay from the detention prison on Ireland Island, they fell on their knees and begged not to be sent on her. They seemed to have had a premonition – but of course they were taken on board and put in irons. She sailed in the evening with the tide and our band played "Home, Sweet Home" and "Auld Lang Syne", and we all watched her setting more sail until at last she disappeared behind Hamilton Point.' He knocked the ash off his cheroot before concluding the story in a sentence: 'She was never seen again.'

'Never?' gasped the girls. 'Not by anyone at all?'

'Never. Never seen again.'

She left at high tide and the natives, lying idly on the shore in the evening light, watched her go. Van saw the dark palm-trees stirring by the water edge and, among them, fruit-trees with fruits like lights, flame-coloured, bottle-green, acid-yellow, dropping with soft plops from the branches to the ground. On the quay glittered the instruments of the band. The sailors, watching the departure, stood in dark, stiff rows. And on the shore lay the lazy, beautiful natives. She saw the native girls with their hair black as horses' hair, all starred over with purple and sugar-pink flowers. They were brown like milk chocolate and wore skirts of grass. As the ship went, they sang after it. They sat on the shore singing after it like the sirens as though they would draw it back again. Some of them swam after it, making long, slow ripples on the oil-smooth evening waters. They swam and swam, holding wreaths of flowers between them, and singing and question-ing, and answering one another in their singing, and all calling together to the ship. She saw their hair floating out on the water and their wet, lifted faces lit by the last of the sun. And the ship passed out of sound of their singing and the music. It sailed away and away, growing small and black, with the reddening light showing between the black, thread-thin rigging. She felt in it all the uneasiness of premonition. An uneasiness was in the evening light and upon the smooth waters and even over the faces of the watching natives.

'And didn't they find anything at all? Not even a life-belt?'

'Not even a life-belt. A great storm swept the Atlantic at

[37]

that time and lasted for five days. A number of merchant vessels were wrecked and it was surmised that the *Atalanta* went down, too. But it is only a surmise. Of all the hundred and one wooden things – buckets, gratings, life-buoys, hencoops – that would ordinarily float adrift when a ship flounders, not one with the name of the *Atalanta* on it was ever found.'

'Do you think perhaps they all decided to go and live on some nice island they passed?'

'It is just possible,' Uncle Samuel smiled.

'But what do you think really happened?'

'I'm afraid she wasn't a seaworthy ship. She and the *Eurydice* were sister ships, they were built from the same plan, and there must have been a fault in it. Perhaps they were top heavy – anyway, altogether, six hundred young lives were lost on them.' The Admiral sighed again and stared at his cheroot.

Vanessa could still see the ship – but it was very tiny now, so tiny you could only really see it through a telescope. She knew everyone on deck was busy doing things, all working, doing their best, none suspecting except the prisoners trapped in irons below. She caught her breath, suddenly frightened and on the verge of tears.

'It all happened a very long time ago,' said the Admiral. 'More than fifty years ago. I was only a youngster myself.'

'I know. That's why.' The picture of it all was so tiny and unreal! Had it all happened yesterday it would have been life-size, but it happened so long ago the picture was tiny like the receding ship. It was like something passing away and away, soon to be out of sight and never seen again. The sense of the receding and disappearing past frightened her with its pathos.

'But how did they know,' she asked, 'the sailors and the marine that didn't want to be taken?'

'Oh, just some silly idea!'

'But it wasn't a silly idea.'

'No, I suppose it wasn't.'

'If something dreadful were going to happen to me, would I know?'

'Bless my soul, what dreadful thing could happen to a little girl like you?'

Moira, who had been lolling back against the wall saying nothing, now prodded Van with her toe. 'You're an idiot, Van. Really, you're an awful idiot.'

'Are you going to London, too, Uncle Samuel?'

'Well,' admitted the Admiral, 'this is no country, you know, for an old Englishman to end his days in. I've stayed a lot longer than I intended . . . But we'll come back one day. People always come back to places where they've been happy. And you'll be almost a grown-up lady then!'

In spite of her efforts to blink them back, two tears made their way down Vanessa's cheeks.

The Admiral eased himself out of his chair muttering: 'Dear me, dear me!' and started hunting among the papers and ornaments on the mantelpiece. 'Ah!' he said as he found a gold cardboard box. 'The very thing to cure a little girl of her fancies!'

He sat down carefully again into his chair and switched on the reading-lamp at his elbow. The electric light coloured the evening air. With slow precision, his short, plump fingers trembling a little, the Admiral lifted the box-lid, then took off a piece of white paper made to look like lace, then a piece of transparent paper, and discovered two rows of crystallized apricots. Van, anxiously watching him place each covering carefully on the table, squealed as the apricots appeared.

'One for Moira,' said Uncle Samuel, 'and the rest for Vanessa and young Joseph.'

'Oh, but—' began Van.

'It's all right,' said Moira. 'We can easily get lots more. We just send to Dublin for them.'

'Really, do they come from Dublin? How marvellous!' Van sat with the open box on her knees and stared at the rich golden gleam of the apricots. Her fears and premonitions were all forgotten and she laughed as though she belonged to the O'Neil household.

While the Admiral went upstairs to change for dinner, the girls went round the room picking up and examining the curios as though they had not seen them before. When one of the footmen came to the door to tell Vanessa that the carriage was waiting for her, her home had ceased to be a reality to her. But there it was! She had to go back.

The Admiral usually went to the big house for dinner. The girls waited for him and then the three sauntered together through the powdery twilight under the trees. The Admiral was smoking another cheroot and the smell of it mingled with the perfume of the woods so that cheroot smoke was ever afterwards to remind Vanessa of that scene – the trees thinning to reveal the lake, bright as the sky, over which the swans floated like black swans on silver water, the dark grass running up to the house with its lighted windows, and the copper-green of the sky. The tobacco flowers at the wood's edge shone through the darkness. The last of the gnats circled under the trees. She was always to remember it with a sense of loss and of happiness come to an end.

They went round to the front of the house where the carriage stood. Joseph was already sitting in it and Herbert stood with one foot on the step. 'Come on, you women,' they called out to the girls.

'Glad you came,' said Herbert as Van took her seat. 'Joseph and I have had a very decent time.'

'Very decent,' agreed Joseph. 'The ferrets were decent.'

'What does decent mean?' asked Van.

'Good Lord! Don't you know that?' shouted Herbert and he and Joseph laughed together.

The Admiral gave a little wave to the children and a special one to Vanessa, then went into the house. Van looked at the doorway for Charles, but there was no sign of him. Miss Hedley called from the hall that Moira and Herbert must say good-bye quickly and go to bed.

'Good-bye. Good-bye. Good-bye.'

Moira and Herbert stood waving from the top of the steps and Van and Joseph knelt on the carriage seat and waved back until the corner was turned and the carriage passed into the darkness of the trees. When the Clandavy children sat down, they felt suddenly sobered and cold. On the coast road they could see the tide was out and the shore looked grey and cold. In the distance before them the lights of the village flickered through the mist at the hills' foot.

'Does it make you feel sad?' asked Van.

Joseph frowned deeply before he said: 'Yes,' and after a pause: 'I don't like feeling sad. It makes me want to run away.'

'Wouldn't you like to go to London with Moira and Herbert?'

'As though we could, you silly fool! What about Mummy?'

'I know. I was just imagining.' She remembered the apricots and opened the box: 'Look!'

Joseph peered down at them. 'How decent!' he said. 'Can I have one?'

'Of course. They're for both of us.'

[41]

They ate all the apricots before Vanessa remembered: 'We ought to have saved one for Mummy.'

'Yes, we ought.'

'Perhaps she'd like the box.'

'It's a decent box. I'd give it to her.'

The carriage went on gently, almost noiselessly, through the heather-scented and melancholy twilight.

'Did you play with the trains?' asked Vanessa.

'Of course not. We're too big for trains. Herbert has a wig-wam in the woods and we made a Red Indian fire and got apples out of the orchard and cooked them on a string over the fire. Bubbles came out of them. They tasted decent.'

'Did Charles play?'

'Charles? No fear. Herbert says he's got awfully conceited since he went to his old school. He thinks he's too good to play with anyone.'

The carriage turned into their own drive. In the distance they could see the glimmer of an oil-lamp in the library window. The electric dynamo had not been in use for a long time.

'Who can be in the library?' whispered Joseph.

Before they reached the house they could hear their mother's angry voice. When they got down from the carriage, they glanced up at the coachman. He touched his hat and turned the horses and drove off as though he had heard nothing. They stood in the dark porch for some moments listening.

'I suppose we'd better go in,' Joseph whispered.

The library door was open and the lamplight came into the hall. The children stood out of range of it, frightened to be seen and frightened by the sound of movement and panting within. Suddenly their mother's voice broke out again: 'You let her think you had plenty of money, did you? You were deceiving her just as you deceived me! She's just a poor fool like me! She thinks you're unhappy! She thinks you're a martyr to your carping, greedy wife and children. We get all your money and we're still discontented, are we? Not a word about how I was deceived when I married you. Not a word about how you expected me to beg from my brothers until they got sick of it and told me I'd get nothing more unless I left you. Not a word about all that.'

She paused to gasp for breath and the sound of a struggle began again, then there was a rattle of a chair as she must have broken free and fallen against it. 'Now,' she gasped, 'now listen to this! "Darling, darling, if I can make you happy and you can leave them comfortably provided for, let us go—" '

'Give it back to me,' came their father's voice, hoarse and strange. Their mother gave a sharp cry.

Joseph ran forward and Van followed him. Mrs Clandavy was thrust against a bookcase with her hands hidden at her breast. Her face was turned sideways so the children could see her profile, her skin red and shining and her upper teeth holding her lower lip. Denis Clandavy was trying to catch her hands which she held away from him. As the children watched, their parents swung round together so the letter their mother was holding became visible. Denis Clandavy's face was unfamiliar in its fury. Mrs Clandavy cried out again and, seeing the children in the doorway, now called them frantically to help her. Joseph flung himself forward at once and kicked at his father's shins. 'Let my Mummy alone,' he screamed. His fists beat wildly at his father's back. 'Let her alone. Let her alone.'

'Here, Vanessa, take it, take it,' cried Mrs Clandavy, waving the letter out of her husband's reach. Vanessa jumped to take it, but her father, with a vicious swiftness of movement, twisted it from his wife's hand and threw her free. She gave a cry of anger and pain and stood sobbing while Vanessa clung to her. Joseph kicked fiercely at his father, screaming: 'I hate you.' Clandavy pushed him away.

'You swine! You filthy, contemptible, low swine!' cried Mrs Clandavy. With the children after her, she swung round and rushed from the room. As the children were crowded back in the doorway, their father called them: 'Vanessa, Joseph.'

Joseph, his face distorted, turned and shrieked: 'Damn you, damn you, damn you!' and rushed on after his mother.

'Vanessa,' there was a sort of pleading in her father's voice that made her pause in spite of herself. She looked at him.

'Come, Vanessa,' called Mrs Clandavy, who was running up the stairs to her room.

'Vanessa, stay for one moment.'

She stood in the doorway, looking miserably at him, drawn both to go and to stay.

'Vanessa,' he said gently. 'If ever you have in your possession a letter or paper that might hurt or damage another person, burn it at once.'

He lifted off the white funnel of the lamp and held the corner of the letter to the flames. It blackened and curled as the flame crept over it.

She knew he was wicked and wrong, she knew he had lied about them and deceived someone, and she wanted to cry.

Joseph's voice called her from the landing. From farther away her mother's voice echoed him: 'Come here, Vanessa, come to me.'

Vanessa looked at her father and backed away slowly and uncertainly. He was staring at the burnt paper and said nothing.

'Vanessa,' called Joseph.

She moved out of her father's sight, then ran upstairs. As she went, she saw the white movement of Dorothy's nightgown on the upper landing. Mrs Clandavy was lying sobbing on her bed. She raised herself as Vanessa came in and demanded: 'What did he say to you? What did he *dare* to say?'

'Nothing. He burnt the paper.' Vanessa felt she could not say letter, that would be showing she understood too much.

'Did he? Did he, indeed! The treacherous fiend! The deceiver! The cur!' She lay back and sobbed more wildly. The room was almost dark. A film of chill and steely light touched a few things near the window.

Joseph climbed up on to the bed and held to his mother. Vanessa climbed up on the other side and buried her face against her mother's back. Together, they sobbed themselves to sleep.

London, 1938.

Two Birthdays

Two Birthdays

The colour of the afternoon sun had begun to deepen. The picnickers decided they could wait no longer. It was past tea-time; the grass would be getting heavy with dew and the party spoilt.

'I'm thinking,' said O'Shea, the bank-clerk, 'I'm thinking it's a pity you asked them.'

'I knew you were thinking that,' said Mrs Cooney. 'I asked them because I was sorry for them never going out or seeing a soul. And now her husband's a year gone and she's free to enjoy herself if she wants to.'

'Are you sure, Mrs Cooney, she accepted? Are you sure?'

'I am,' said Mrs Cooney.

Down on the deep, darkening incurve of water under the trees the boats lay like melon-pips. The tea-baskets were on board. The half-dozen friends, standing up in the sunlight, stopped chatting and began to look round restlessly.

'We'll go on, then,' said O'Shea. 'We'll leave her a boat and if she can't row, Nolan can bring her along.'

'I'll do that,' the boatman nodded.

Before anyone could stop him by disagreeing, O'Shea went half running, half sliding down the grass, his short, neat feet shooting out at an angle on either side of him. He let his breath out with relief when he heard the others following. In a few moments the two boats were pushing out, wobbling until everyone was settled and the oars symmetrical in the row-locks. For a moment the blades lay like wings on the smooth, evening waters, then the rowers started a race towards their destination.

They were out of sight before Mrs Clandavy, with Joseph and Vanessa before her, came bending her lean height under the willow trees. Joseph, his arms and legs outgrowing his old sailor suit, was imitating a railway train. He stopped abruptly and his face, with its lingering baby look became strained, then collapsed altogether. 'There's no one here,' he cried.

'Be quiet,' his mother commanded automatically.

Nolan made a dramatic appearance out of his hut among the bushes and touched his cap to the black-clad widow. He said: 'They're away off, for it was getting late. But there's a boat left here for you and if you can't row, I'll take you there myself.'

Mrs Clandavy scarcely glanced at him. 'We'll not bother,' she said, 'it's too late.' She turned as though she would walk away at once.

'Oh, Mummy,' whispered Van.

Joseph stared down at the boat left for them, then folding his arms on a level with his face and burying his eyes in them, he began to sob. Through his sobs he choked out: 'It's your fault we were late. You wouldn't get ready. I knew we wouldn't go. I knew. I knew.'

Mrs Clandavy clicked her tongue. 'This boy has to spoil everything,' she said.

'If I didn't spoil it, we wouldn't have it.'

'You're not late at all,' Nolan joined in soothingly. 'I'll row you there in no time.'

'If I want to go, I can row myself.' Mrs Clandavy stared

with a flushed indignant expression down the river for some moments while the children watched her anxiously, then she asked: 'Where have they gone?'

Nolan opened his mouth, but shut it without saying anything. He followed the direction of her stare and shaded his eyes as though trying to see where the rowers had gone, then at last he replied: 'They'll be at Menlo. That's the place for a picnic.'

'Menlo, Menlo,' Joseph started clapping his hands and jumping into the air now he knew his mother was capitulating, 'Menlo's the place for a picnic.'

Van got first into the boat and seated herself in the stern.

'But I want to steer,' said Joseph.

'Well, you can't,' said Van, 'because I'm going to.'

'Mummy, Mummy, I want to steer.'

'Let Joseph steer,' said Mrs Clandavy.

'Oh, but, Mummy, why? Why can't I?'

'You can sit nicely in the bows.'

'But I don't want to. Why should I? If Joseph can steer, why can't I?'

'Because Joseph is a boy and you are a girl. You'll soon be growing into a young lady.'

'What difference does that make?'

'All the difference in the world.'

'Yes, but what difference?'

'Don't ask questions.'

The boat was pushed off and settled into the water with Joseph holding the rudder lines and Van sitting glumly in the bows. Mrs Clandavy handled the oars skilfully and with a strength that would have surprised any onlooker but her children, who took whatever she did for granted. Tears were still glistening on Joseph's cheeks as he beamed across at Van. She put out her tongue at him and his expression changed to surprise. He had already forgotten she had cause for complaint.

Mrs Clandavy, seeing Joseph's expression change, said: 'Stop that, Vanessa, I'm very annoyed with you.'

'Why are you annoyed with me. Joseph wanted to steer and he's steering.'

'I don't want to argue with you.'

'I think you're stupid,' said Van.

Mrs Clandavy did not seem to hear. She pulled on her oars once or twice, then said slowly and reflectively: 'Yes, I am stupid. I have sacrificed everything for my children and they tell me I'm a fool.'

The Corrib lay pale in the late light. Some monks in a dinghy were trying to catch the wind in their sail. They tacked from side to side and soon passed the rowing-boat. Joseph shouted and waved to them. When they had got ahead they waved to him and smiled cautiously, avoiding looking at the woman and girl. When they were out of sight, silence came down on the scarcely moving, trafficless water. The shadows of the grass blades stretched over the meadows on either side. Mrs Clandavy's rowing slowed – she realized she had not the strength she had had as a girl – but they moved easily and with a dream-floating quiet.

Van, caught in a complex emotional web of resentment, guilt and jealousy, stared down into the glass-green depths of the water. She knew she had been wrong in adding to her mother's unhappiness. She seemed always to be adding to it, and she resented its being there all the time to put her in the wrong. She could not understand why her mother sorrowed so much about her father's death when during his lifetime they had done nothing but quarrel.

Nearly all the quarrels had been about money. The worst ones had been before they sold Clandavy House to the man who thought of starting an hotel. After they moved to one of the empty houses on the Galway seafront, the debts had been paid and the children sent to school. They had lived very well for a few months – and then it had all started again. Vanessa could remember her father flinging out one night into the downpour of rain and not coming home. The next day had been Mrs Clandavy's birthday and her elder brother in Edinburgh had sent her a five-pound note. That must be exactly a year ago, for today was again Mrs Clandavy's birthday. Van could remember how her mother had stood by the table and smoothed out a piece of paper that rattled like tinfoil.

'What is it?' Joseph had asked.

'Money,' said their mother. Suddenly she looked up from the note and asked sharply and accusingly: 'Where's your father?' Van went to his room and found he had not slept there. 'Then I'll go,' said their mother, 'I'll go to Edinburgh.'

'Can we come, too?' asked Joseph.

After a long pause Mrs Clandavy put the note away in her bag and said: 'I would leave him if it weren't for you two children. At any time I could go to my brother's home and be welcome. I only stay here for your sake.'

But, Van reflected as she stared at the water, when their father was dead and Uncle James had written to ask them all to Edinburgh, her mother had refused to go. She said she could not leave Ireland, although she had always said she hated it so much.

When the children returned from school that morning a year ago, they stood listening in the porch to hear whether or not their father had come home. If he were home there would be a fury of voices and banging doors, all the usual uproar glancing from room to room. But there was silence. They would probably get something to eat. Actually, their mother had bought special things with the five-pound note and was waiting for them. There had been tomatoes and tongue in a glass dish. When Van and Joseph exclaimed with delight, their mother said:

'Why shouldn't we enjoy ourselves, too? There's no knowing where he's gone off to. We'll go to the cinema.'

That had startled them into silence. They had never been to the famous cinema that had opened in the Town Hall. They stared at her and Van whispered: 'Do you really mean it?'

Yes, she assured them, and told them not to waste time over their food or they would be late. They started eating the marvellous tongue with the jelly round the edges and the bright, little tomatoes, and were all talking and laughing – and then, just when everything was so wonderful and their mother for once was being so jolly and friendly, the door opened and their father came in. Mrs Clandavy's face hardened at once. The children knew everything was spoiled. Joseph had caught at his mother's hand to try and divert her attention, to try and hold to things as they had been, but she would not look at him. Very stiff and tall, she stood up.

Her husband had wandered across the room and thrown himself into a chair. He sat with his head down on his chest while she looked at him. The children, worried and miserable, felt sorry for him, but they wanted to go to the pictures.

Joseph had tugged at his mother's hand again and whispered: 'Come on, Mummy. Let's go to the cinema,' but Mrs Clandavy snatched her hand away and said to her husband: 'Where have you been?'

After a pause he said: 'To Spiddal.'

'Why? Why to Spiddal?'

'To see Harry Tufnell.'

'You wasted money going to Spiddal to see Harry Tufnell?'

[54]

'I walked there and back.'

'Did you now? And why? Why, may I ask?'

'He owed me some money.' He put his hand slowly into his coat and drew out a pound note. He let it fall on to the arm of his chair.

His wife looked at it and drew her lips down. 'You can keep it,' she said, 'you can lend it to one of your other friends, the same as you lend every penny we get.'

'Oh, for God's sake!' He had turned his face away and his cheek had looked like a bleached bone balanced on the sinews of his neck.

To the children the pound note on their father's chair-arm looked small and paltry when they thought of the big five-pound note, but somehow it made them feel more sorry for their father. They felt like crying. It did not seem possible ever to enjoy anything. Mrs Clandavy, too, was looking at the pound note and suddenly she caught her breath. She dropped into her chair and put her face into her hands. The children ran to embrace her at once and stared accusingly at their father. He seemed unaware of all of them as he lay exhausted in his chair. Joseph made one more attempt. He whispered: 'Let's go, Mummy. Let's go to the cinema.'

'Leave me alone,' cried Mrs Clandavy, 'we're not going now.'

'Oh, Mummy,' Van's voice had broken with disappointment.'

'Mummy, Mummy,' Joseph had started to wail.

'God!' their father sat upright, 'what a hell! No peace, no quiet, no rest—' He broke off in a fit of coughing.

'Blame yourself for it,' Mrs Clandavy shouted at him as he doubled up coughing in the chair.

Suddenly she said with decision: 'Yes, we shall go to the cinema. We'll go. Perhaps he walked to Spiddal. Perhaps he did!' Then she noticed her husband's face. Van had been sent running for Mrs Cooney and Mrs Cooney telephoned for a doctor.

Van, sitting now in the stern of the boat, held a sleek fold of water in her hand and watched her pink fingers blanch beneath the glazing of green water. Joseph, watching for their destination, was silenced by the autumn quiet. They passed the ruins of Clanrickard Castle which stood with a naked, unclaimed look on the flat meadowland beside the river. None of them noticed the boats of the picnickers drawn into the opposite bank or heard the distant scratch of voices from among the trees half a mile away.

'There's a coot,' whispered Joseph. Mrs Clandavy looked at the little black, floating bird with its bald pate, and smiled. Van felt over her mother the sadness of the sweet and delicate light. She remembered why they had been allowed to come to the picnic. She said: 'It's your birthday, Mummy.'

'How old are you?' asked Joseph.

'Thirty-two,' said Mrs Clandavy.

'Years?' asked Joseph, his eyes widening, 'thirty-two years?'

'Yes.'

Joseph looked at Van to see her reaction, but Van knew it was rude to comment on anyone's age, so they said nothing. The sun crept down the unbroken sheen of the sky. There was a glow and tranquillity on everything. At last, round the corner, the Menlo ruins appeared, deep in trees and much more friendly than Clanrickard. They tied their boat to the little jetty and climbed up the steps to lawns that were lost in nettle, docken and weeds. There was complete silence everywhere.

'But they aren't here,' said Joseph.

'It doesn't matter,' said their mother. Van agreed, but for

some minutes Joseph was not sure. As the children climbed over the fallen walls into the ruined banqueting hall, he kept looking for the others, but he soon forgot them. There were young trees growing inside the hall, and branches and creepers had found their way in through the large window spaces. 'Do come in, Mummy,' shouted Van, but Mrs Clandavy preferred to wander off by herself.

'She never does anything with us,' said Joseph.

'Sometimes I think she doesn't love us very much,' said Van.

'Well,' said Joseph after long reflection, 'I don't think she does, but I think she loves me best.'

They wandered around without speaking after that, making their way through the fallen rooms to the courtyard, where they parted the rich foliage to look into the stables.

'The horses were all saved from the fire,' said Joseph with satisfaction. 'The men from the village came and saved the horses.'

All the Galway children knew the story of Menlo. Van took it up at once: 'But they wouldn't save *her*. They let her run screaming round from window to window, and they wouldn't move to help her they hated her so much. When they couldn't find her body they said the devil had taken it.'

The children, suddenly nervous in the green gloom, darted away to find their mother. They found her sitting on a stretch of riverside grass where wild raspberries grew. She had a handful of berries she was eating slowly one by one.

'What's the matter with you children?' she said.

'When they couldn't find her body, they said the devil took it,' explained Joseph.

Mrs Clandavy did not ask him what he was talking about, but sat looking towards the sunset as though she had not heard. The children threw themselves on the grass beside her.

The sky looked very wide and high, its tea-rose colour reflected in the glassy river. The grass fringes of the banks hung darkly over the unmoving edges of the water. From somewhere in the distance came a sound of oars in rowlocks.

Mrs Clandavy spoke quietly as though the evening were damping her voice. 'I remember when I was a little girl,' she said, 'we used to go each year to a house in the Highlands where there was a loch. We had a rowing-boat of our own. All the winter it lay upside-down on the shore of the loch and when we came in the spring we used to paint it a different colour – one year blue, another year red, and once yellow with a white stripe. We used to row out to a little island where there were wild bees.'

'With honey?' asked Joseph.

'Beautiful dark brown honey tasting of heather. My brother James would put on one of my straw hats and one of mother's veils and go to the island and smoke the bees away.'

'How? With a pipe?'

'No. He burnt brown paper and made a lot of smoke and the bees would all fly away, and then he'd take the honey. We used to swim on warm days, but the water was always icy cold. We'd jump in from the boat and when we came to the surface, we'd feel quite stunned.'

Van watched her mother, afraid that some question or comment might make her stop speaking and retreat from them. Van could see the lake with the island and the little boys and the girl jumping into the cold water. She could see their heads come to the surface panting and laughing. It was strange to think the little girl was now their mother, and their mother had been a little girl. She had never spoken of her childhood before except to say: 'When I was a child I was always considerate,' or well behaved, or obedient, or some such, so they had never really believed she had ever been a

[58]

child. When Van thought of the little girl who jumped into the loch and who helped paint the boat, her mother seemed at once more real and more mysterious. Van moved slightly towards her, filled with tenderness for her, believing that now she must feel the same for them or she would not talk to them like this.

'My mother was alive at that time,' said Mrs Clandavy. 'I cannot remember her very well because I was the youngest. I was only eight when she died, but I know my father loved her very much. He never married again. She must have been happy . . . but perhaps she wasn't. There's no telling.' Mrs Clandavy propped herself up on her elbow and her lips hardened. 'When you are young,' she said, 'you look forward to so much. You think you'll never be fool enough to waste your life as others waste theirs. You think you know how to avoid the disappointments that come to others, and you'll do the things other people want to do and can't. But you make just the same mistakes in the end.'

Van and Joseph avoided one another's eyes. Some moments passed while their mother watched the flowing river. Suddenly Joseph jumped up and started running round in circles and making a noise like a train. Van said to herself: 'Oh, don't, Joseph.'

Mrs Clandavy turned her head sharply. 'Stop that nonsense, Joseph. You're becoming a big boy now. Can't you keep still for a moment? Sit down.'

'I can't,' he said. 'I've got to go round and round until I run down.'

His mother got to her feet and dusted her black skirts. 'We'll go now.' She took Van's hand. The two walked down to the boat, leaving Joseph still running in circles. He came after them at once. 'I've run down, I've run down,' he shouted. They took no notice of him. The sun had set. When they pushed out into the moss-dark greenness of the river, the night was falling quickly and a cold wind was stirring the leaves. The children shivered.

'We stayed too long at Menlo,' said Mrs Clandavy.

It was almost dark when they reached the boathouse. They could see the glimmer of the shirt of the boatman whom they had kept waiting. All the other boats were drawn up on to the grass. In the air there was a smell of leaves that seemed to Van full of memories of something she could not recall. She caught her mother's hand and held to it.

As the children, half-asleep, walked home with their mother, they hid in her skirts away from the cold, singing wind. Out in the bay the lights of a ship moved slowly.

'Look, there's a liner,' said Joseph. 'You can see the port-holes.'

'It's going to America,' said Mrs Clandavy. 'It won't sight land again until it reaches New York.'

Van thought of the people on the ship going so far away. She was troubled and frightened when she thought of the number of people on the earth and of the distant lands she might never see, and she clung to her mother. As they turned into the dark crescent formed by the houses, Mrs Clandavy put an arm round each of the children and they felt come from her a sweetness they seldom knew.

'One day,' said Joseph, 'I'll go to America and take you with me.'

'And me, too,' said Van.

Mrs Clandavy did not reply. She took her arms away to find the front-door key. The children looked up and saw she was staring straight ahead towards their house. As she turned into the gate and hurried up the drive, they felt she had forgotten them.

London, 1938.

A Case of Injury

A Case of Injury

It was one of those mornings in autumn when the cold is exhilarating. It had been raining all night and the uneven paving-stones looked like the washed flags of a kitchen. The wind smelt of the river. I turned off the main road into a crooked side-street where some men were unloading barrels from a lorry and lowering them down a runway into the cellar of a public-house. A smell like salt-fish came up from the cellar and a strong tarry smell from the ropes with which the men controlled the barrels. I stood for some minutes watching the men moving through the shadowless, grey atmosphere. In those days I had no interest in words at all. I could be so absorbed by something I was watching that I would not hear what was said to me. When my arm was touched, I looked round and saw a young man whose mouth still had the movement of speech about it. I knew he was repeating what he had said before, and I flushed slightly in apology.

'Wouldn't you be one of the young ladies from Bally-donald?' he asked.

'Yes, I used to live there.' When I told him my name, he nodded as though he were familiar with it.

'I grew up on your grandfather's estate,' he said. 'My father was head gardener there.'

'He wasn't my grandfather. He was my mother's cousin. I haven't been there for years.'

'Perhaps you've heard of me – Nick Grew – I ran away from home and went to England. That's why I talk like an Englishman.'

'I would have known you were an Irishman anywhere,' I said, remembering nothing about him. 'And now you're working in Dublin?' I asked.

'No, I'm looking for work. I've been here a month or more looking for work and not a thing offered me. They're a clanny lot. They all think I'm English, and when I say I'm from the north they say that's worse. Life's hard.'

'I suppose it is.' I had started moving away from the stares of the men with the barrels and the young man kept up with me. He was carrying a cap of loud check stuff, very dirty, and the wind was blowing through his hair. He was a short, dark young man of a type found in all parts of Ireland where there is Spanish blood. It was obvious from his bearing that in England he had been thought a handsome man, but I knew the Irish, with their eighteenth-century fastidiousness, would look down on him as a ruffian. The side-street turned into a lane and ran towards the river.

'Now, your father might be able to help me,' he said.

'I'm sorry,' I said, 'but my family is in England.'

'You're not telling me you're here alone.'

'Yes. I'm a student at the art school.'

He waited until we reached the quay, then he said suddenly: 'I suppose you wouldn't lend me two and a tanner?'

'I haven't got it,' I said.

He laughed. 'I'll let you have it back. I promise.'

'Yes, I'm sure of that – but I really mean I have no money.'

'I've had no breakfast,' he said.

'Neither have I.'

He laughed again, but had nothing more to say for a hundred yards. We were walking along the quays towards the brewery. I kept looking for a clock because I had a Life Class at ten. He began to whistle in a jaunty way, swinging his cap round like a plate between his fingers. Suddenly he stopped and said: 'Did you mean what you said about having no money?'

'Yes.'

'What about your da? – he must have plenty. Won't he send you some?'

'He hasn't got plenty. If I went home they'd keep me, but if I want to stay here I have to keep myself.'

'How do you do that?'

'I have a scholarship grant of a hundred pounds, and I work in the evenings from five to eight. I do tracing for architects.'

'Had a bad week like, this week?'

'I had to buy some paints.'

'You're a funny young lady!'

'Why?'

'You answer questions.'

'What do you expect me to do?'

'Tell me to mind my own business. I suppose you wouldn't come and have a bite with me tonight?'

'I don't think I can.'

'Ah!' he burst out. 'You see, now! You haven't a penny, but you think yourself too good to eat with me!'

'I don't know what money has to do with it.'

'Don't you? If I had money, I'd be a big man by this time. If I had money and could take you to Jammet's, you'd jump at it.'

'I don't know that I would. As you haven't any money, why should you ask me?'

'I'll get some. I promise you if you come you'll have a proper meal.'

'It's difficult – I always eat with a friend.'

'A gentleman friend?'

'No, the girl I live with.'

'Bring her along.'

I was apologetic towards Rosalie when I told her what had happened. 'The thing is – we might be able to help him. Perhaps he would do as a model for the Life Class.'

Rosalie was ten years my senior. She had grown up in a small English country town and attended a day school. As her parents would not let her leave home to study art, she had waited until she inherited some money on her thirtieth birthday. Then, afraid to go alone to Paris, she had come to Dublin to be as far from her family as possible. She was a second-year student, but had not yet passed into the Life Class. She offered to rent me a room in her flat as soon as I arrived at the school. Being both a student and a wage-earner, I had little time for people, so for months she was my only friend. I soon treated her as someone younger and less experienced than myself. It was a long time before I discovered she resented this. She was a long, plain, light-haired girl with glasses. At first she looked prim and self-regarding: later one saw she was forlorn behind her steady, superior smile.

She giggled at me. 'Fancy letting a young man pick you up!'

'He remembered me from my infancy.'

'Most romantic!'

'You won't think so when you see him.'

She met me outside the office where I had done an evening's work for five shillings, and we took the tram to O'Connell Bridge. When I saw him standing there under a lamp, I started to apologize again but Rosalie said sharply: 'He's not bad. What a snob you are!'

Nick Grew looked at us both as though we were one person. 'Well, I didn't think you young ladies would turn up. A change for you to be going out with a chap like me!'

'We don't usually go out with chaps at all,' Rosalie giggled, and Grew gave her a look and I saw him separate her from me for the first time.

He took us to a restaurant in a side-street opposite the Nelson Column. There was a large upstairs room with dancing at one end. As soon as we sat down, Grew, with an elaborate courtesy, asked me to dance. When I said truthfully that I could not dance, he turned from me impatiently and said to Rosalie: 'Come on,' as though he were sure of her. I watched them through the haze of tobacco smoke. Grew danced with his backside out and his head forward as though used to leaning over his partner. As Rosalie was the taller, his head butted her shoulder and her face hung vaguely over him with a silly smile. The waiter brought three plates of eggs and chips. I started eating mine before they returned to the table.

'There,' Grew pointed at me and said accusingly to the world, 'the first food she's had today.'

'Well.' Rosalie became prim. 'We've agreed not to lend each other money. We've got to cut our coats, you know.'

'Port and lemon?' asked Grew. 'Waiter, three port and lemons.'

When they had been dancing for about two hours, I left a note of excuse on the table and went home. Some time in the middle of the night, I awoke and heard them coming up the stairs. Had they remained in the sitting-room I would have heard their voices. When their voices were cut off and I knew they had gone into Rosalie's room, I sat up with surprise. But I could do no more than lie down again.

Next morning I hurried out of the house and had coffee in the Oriental Café. I did not see Rosalie until luncheon-time when I went to our usual teashop. In she came, making her way between the tables, very tall, stooping slightly to hide it, her face unusually pink. Her expression became smug when she caught sight of me.

'Well?' I said.

'Ah!' She sat down, picked up the menu and peered at it. She could not concentrate on it and threw it down again. 'What are you having?'

'Sardines on toast.'

'I'll have the same, but I'll have some soup, too.' She opened and shut her handbag, then reopened it and took out a nail-file. She tried to get some oil-paint out of her finger-nails, but put the file back in a moment. In the end she burst out: 'Nick came back with me last night.'

'I know.'

'But you don't know everything. He's amazing. He's really wonderful, he's so *passionate*.' She started a description of their night together that made me worried with embarrassment. It was not that she was frank – we all went out of our way to be frank in those days – but that she was quivering with excitement. I knew she was describing the whole thing to relive it. As she talked – moist, hot and breathless – I could not look at her. I saw two shop-girls wandering round looking for a table and I willed them to come over to ours. When they took the seats opposite us, I let my breath out. I thought: 'This will shut her up.' But she did not even notice them. She began describing how he had prevented her from taking a bath. The attention of the two girls was fixed on her at once. Had she been saying nothing she would have attracted it by the heightened atmosphere around her. I kicked at her foot and made an eyebrow towards them. She gave a giggle, so I knew she was enjoying their bewilderment. Her descriptions became more graphic and I began to fear the girls would complain to the waitress, but they only sat with fixed stares, sometimes exchanging glances to confirm they were both really hearing what they heard. I began to wish they would go, but they stayed to the end. As though for their benefit, Rosalie started repeating everything again, and I stood up, with the excuse of a class at two-thirty.

After that Rosalie began to take her meals with Grew at the upstairs restaurant. I saw her between classes, but she had become more coy about her experiences. She tittered and nodded and moved her eyes mischievously behind her glasses. Later she became serious. She was discovering, she said, how sensitive Grew was and how easily hurt. He had strange moods; strange fits of petulance and temper that, for her, proved him to be no ordinary man. She said: 'If you ask me, I'd say he has seeds of greatness in him.' Then she began excusing him for faults, which she did not describe, by saying how hard his life had been.

I was only surprised that the relationship continued so long. I could not understand what he was up to, but it seemed explained one day when she said she had lent him twenty pounds. Two days later she lent him fifty pounds to buy a secondhand car which he said had been offered him by a pal. He told her he had been an engineer and the purchase of this car was somehow to give him 'a fresh start in life'. When she lent him a second fifty pounds, I must have shown my surprise.

'Well,' she said, 'and why not? I don't mind paying for something if I want it. If there's something I want, I'll pay a good price for it – that's if I *really* want it. I've always been like that.'

[69]

'Are you sure he's honest?'

'Yes, I'm sure. The other day we went to Glendalough in the car and it broke down. It's always breaking down. He said he could mend it. He spent ages tinkering about with it, but he couldn't get it right.'

'You said he was an engineer.'

'Yes, but engineers don't mend motor-cars. And what do you think! He suddenly banged down the hood and started crying. I mean, really crying. He sat down on the running-board and cried like a little boy. Anyone like that must be honest.'

It was scarcely a week after that that her whole attitude changed. I could tell as she came into the Antique Class that something was wrong. When, later, I mentioned Grew a spasm of disgust crossed her face.

'I'm sick of him,' she said.

'Why, what has happened?'

'Nothing. I just suddenly saw him as he really is – a conceited, little vulgarian. He's . . . he's a twerp.'

'But he's a working man – one can't call him a vulgarian.'

'Yes, he is. He's vulgar because he pretends to be what he isn't. And his sensuality! – it disgusts me. It really disgusts me. It suddenly made me feel unclean. I've told him definitely that I've finished. I've told him he needn't try and be a nuisance. I won't see him again.'

I thought probably he had insulted her in some way or found another girl. I scarcely believed her next day when she said he had gone off in the car to find work at Cork in order to forget about her.

'And good riddance,' she said. 'It's all right being democratic – you're all democratic in theory, but I've tried it and I know all about it.

We began to eat together again, but she would not talk

about Grew. If he were mentioned, she made a face as though reminded of something distasteful.

One evening as we were walking home late, I thought I heard someone following us and looked behind. 'That was Grew,' I said.

'Where?' Rosalie swung round with an anger I had never before seen in her, but the man had disappeared. She said breathlessly: 'If he speaks to me again, I'll give him in charge. I mean it – I'll give him in charge.'

That night I was wakened by someone thumping the front door. We lived alone above a lock-up shop and the knocks from the street came echoing up the bare, wooden stairway and filled our flat. I heard Rosalie go into the sitting-room and throw up the front window. She shouted something, shut the window sharply and went back with a quick, heavy tread to her room. The knocking went on quietly at intervals for some time after, but she made no other response.

When I went down early next morning, I found Grew sitting on the doorstep, his face buried in his arms. I shook him awake. For some moments he did not raise his head, then he did so sharply with a completely awake and hopeful expression that faded at once when he saw me. His eyes were red with crying.

I said: 'It's no good worrying Rosalie. She says she'll give you in charge if you don't leave her alone.' When I got him to his feet and persuaded him to walk with me, I asked: 'What have you done to upset her?'

'Nothing.' His manner was dramatic, yet convincing: 'She changed all of a sudden. I loved her. I still love her. You see, she's a lady – that means a lot to me.'

I took him to a café, where he gulped down boiling coffee and said between gulps:

'I'll pay her back, I'll pay her every penny. If she despises me, I'll not be beholden to her. Not me. I only took her money because I thought she loved me.'

He said he had a plan to drive the car to Belfast, sell it there and return to Liverpool, where he believed he could find work.

'Yes, I'd do that,' I said.

He gazed out of the café window. 'You're sure it's no good hanging around in case she . . .'

'No good at all.'

He nodded. I knew he had been convinced before he asked. He lifted his cup, swilled round the dregs and swallowed them. 'I'll go,' he said. 'I'll show her. Her and her money!' He put down the cup and looked towards me without seeing me, his eyes black and wretched: 'I'm an injured man,' he said.

I watched him get into the little ramshackle car.

'If it weren't beneath me,' he said when he had persuaded the engine to start, 'I'd sue her for breach of promise.' He gave me a last nod.

I nodded, too, in sympathy and watched him drive away. Although he forgot to return the money, I still think of him as an injured man.

London, 1939.

A Visit

A Visit

My brother used to say: 'The first thing I remember is falling downstairs. You pushed me. I had to climb up farther than you so you couldn't push me again.' I suppose he thought that accounted for the ambition that kept him working night after night so that all the work might be behind him, so he would find himself at last on a pinnacle of security. When he sat for his last examination, he was two years younger than any of the other candidates. He passed brilliantly. My mother was proud of him. Then one night he came downstairs with a grey face and silently held out his handkerchief. We all looked at the fresh red stain on the linen. Less than a year later he was dead. My mother, who had travelled with him, wrote to me from Switzerland: 'My poor Andrew, my poor boy, if he had been less ambitious to make money for me he might have been alive now.'

My father was a draughtsman. He drew very beautifully in pencil or ink – animals, flowers, houses with gardens overhanging the sea – but there was no market for his work. He could not make a living. My mother had been one of eight girls, so very little of the family money came to her. All I remember now is being taken across the sea to a place where the air was dark and cold and it was always raining. We had left our Cornish cottage for Belfast, where my father had found work as a designer in a linen factory.

My mother at once accused us and made excuses to us: 'You can live on nothing until you have children – then you must face your responsibilities.' We knew we must blame ourselves. Because of us our parents had had to leave their friends and the sunshine and come to this town.

'You must have money,' my mother said. 'You must work and be independent. If you have money and independence, you can look the world in the face.'

She had never belonged to the artist crowd into which my father had taken her. She came of an Ulster family, once land-owning and respected, and she talked of money and in-dependence as exiles talk of home. My beautiful little brother with his fair skin, his large grey eyes and his hair like gauze round his head, stared at her and listened. His mouth, that was sensitive yet could look inflexible, grew strained in response to the effort she was provoking in him. She said: 'When you're in need, you will find friends nowhere. The world is a harsh, cruel, lonely place when you have no money.'

We knew all about the world. It was outside our window: the black river crawling under the drizzle of rain; the wet cobbles; the dirty pavements; the stale fishy smell from the docks; the women with starved and bitter faces beneath their shawls; the cold – the irritating chilliness of summer and the knife-edged winter cold; and the harsh-voiced school-children whom we, the aliens, were always fighting.

My father sat in his little drawing-office at the top of a tall, brick building and drew with a fine pen the shamrocks and harps and roses that were embroidered on tea-cloths or woven into the damask tablecloths. When he could get away with his sketch-book, he took the bus down the Hollywood Road towards Bangor or up to the Cave Hill. He did not take us with him. I know now he did not want to be reminded by our presence of the obligations of reality. He had enough of them at home. When it was obvious that he was going to become neither rich nor famous, my mother began to treat him with contempt. We admired and imitated her. She it was who had the knowledge of the frightening outside world. She knew the tricks with which to combat it. She could advise us. She knew the forces that would aid our escape from this town. In return we must earn escape for her. She was our suffering mother who had come to this place for our sakes; we must work for hers.

One day she said to my father: 'I think we should take the children to see old Lady Moxton. She might take a fancy to them.'

We knew what that meant. We appreciated the cunning and the need to get the better of life. Lady Moxton was a name in our house and a mysterious power behind it. She was a member of my mother's family – the only successful one, for she had married the director of a linen house. It was she who had used 'influence' to get father his position. If, in caprice, she cared to say a word against him, we would all be flung out into the bottomless pit of poverty. We were terrified at the prospect of meeting her, but knew we must face it. She had by inheritance the things we must achieve for ourselves.

On the day arranged for the visit, Andrew had one of his bronchial colds. He lay with the long spout of the steam-kettle poking through the rails of his bed. His eyes shone amusement at me because I had to face Lady Moxton without him.

My mother and I caught a tram-car that took us out past the wet, green gardens of large, red houses to the edge of the town. The rain stopped for a short time. The sun trickled out. We picked our way down an unmade road to the gates of

Moxton House. In its day it had been a great house entertaining all the Ulster gentry, but Lady Moxton had been a widow and bed-ridden for years and the façade was falling into decay. We walked up a long drive between jungles of vegetations. In the south where hundreds of houses like this lay deserted or burnt to the ground, it would have been unnoticed; but here in the north people whispered to my parents about this neglect as they might about a failure of morals. Had they been allowed, as we were, to enter, they might have been appeased by the sight of the furniture everywhere under dust-sheets and a path of yellowing newspapers protecting the carpets that covered the stairs to Lady Moxton's room. A smell of dusty plush filled the house. On the stairs my breath gave out and I sagged down on my knees. My mother pulled me on.

'I'm going to be sick,' I whispered.

'Oh,' she wailed, as far as she could wail in a whisper. 'Haven't I enough to bear?'

'It's all right, it's all right,' I swallowed, bracing myself, putting a stop to her agony as quickly as I could.

She gave me a furious look, but was helpless, as the housekeeper was now opening the double doors into Lady Moxton's room. A shaft of sunlight, swimming with dust, hid the interior from us. From behind it a voice spoke. The housekeeper hurried to the window, pulled a blind and shut the sun out.

Through the oil-green shadow we saw Lady Moxton lying in a brass bedstead beneath an untidy heap of covers. I was almost overcome by the smell of drugs and urine. Two suspicious eyes, ringed with black paint, were fixed upon me. I took a step backwards. My mother pushed me forward again.

'Say "How d'you do" to Lady Moxton,' said my mother in an unfamiliar, sugary tone.

'Don't stare like that, child,' commanded a very deep voice. 'That child's an imbecile, Eleanor.'

'No, no. Miranda's only very shy. Don't stare, Miranda dear.'

I went on staring, feeling I had no power to move my eyes. I was fascinated by the colour of Lady Moxton's hair that was piled shapelessly on her head. It was purple and cherry-red on top and a sallow grey at the roots. The face beneath had the rough texture of the false faces we bought for Guy Fawkes Day. It was a deathly white but scarlet on the cheeks and lips, and the eyes flickered acutely aware. I managed somehow to look away. I fixed my gaze on the little electric fire that was eating up the stale air of the room.

As soon as we sat down, my mother started talking about the difficulty of bringing up two children on my father's salary. Poverty, she said quite untruthfully, was not a thing to which she was used. Belfast offered her nothing, nothing. The climate did not suit Andrew, who had a weak chest. She talked in a tone of bright resignation I had never heard before.

'This is a fine, bracing climate,' Lady Moxton broke in harshly. 'That boy of yours is a weakling.'

I kept raising my eyes and looking at things in the room, but I did not dare to look at Lady Moxton again. The bamboo table was covered with medicine bottles. I imagined the sweetish, powdery taste of the white one and the acid taste of the mahogany-red. There was a plate with a smear of jam and a jammy spoon that reminded me I was feeling sick. On another bamboo table was a crowd of dusty cacti and geraniums. There was an embroidered linen coverlet straggling half on the bed and half off it. I looked round the walls: on the dirty grey paint with its gilt-edged panels were steel engravings spotted with damp. Over the bed was the picture of a solitary deer lifting its voice in a frozen landscape. I stared at it and shared its desolation.

Suddenly I heard the deep voice say: 'Perhaps I should give the little girl something.' My head jerked towards Lady Moxton and between her lacquer red lips, I saw her false teeth hanging loose from the gums the lips crooked in a smile. My whole body became hot and shivering at my success. Then I became cold.

She made me fetch a black deed-box from among the curls of dust under the bed. I placed it on her knees, then stood and watched her. My mother made me sit down again, but I sat on the very edge of the chair, leaning forward, transformed in anticipation. I watched Lady Moxton's hands – large-boned with a mummy-yellow covering of skin – fumble among the shawls and flannels that muffled her to the chin. She found a key strung on a cord and opened the box. I caught my breath. My mother gave me a furious dig, but I scarcely felt it.

'Sit up properly,' commanded my mother. I straightened my shoulders, but my eyes were fixed on the tangle of jewellery inside the box. The gold was dim, the silver black, the stones glinted through the metal chains like dying stars. I felt this added a value to it all – the antiquity my father prized in furniture.

The hands picked up a thin, gold chain from which hung a little heart of blue enamel. That, I knew, was the right sort of present for me. It must have been the smallest thing in the box, but the hands held to it.

'It's quite valuable,' said Lady Moxton.

I made an appreciative murmur. I knew how important value was.

I waited – but the hands dropped the heart back into the box again. They fumbled and drew out a florid rose of red stones. The hands moved slightly towards me, but passed, withdrew and the rose fell back with the rest. I was trembling with anxiety. Lady Moxton lifted a curb bracelet. She murmured:

'I don't know, I don't know.'

'Dear Lady Moxton, don't worry about the child,' my mother said in a tone that accused me of failure.

Lady Moxton took no notice of her. A ring with a green opal was picked up. I felt a little spasm of wanting it for itself rather than for its value. It went back with the others. Tears stood in my eyes.

'Perhaps another time,' said Lady Moxton, not unkindly. The hands shut the box, locked it and patted it as though it had come intact through an ordeal. She gave a sigh: 'Put it back for me, child. Bring her another time, Eleanor.'

'Next week?'

'No, not next week. I will let you know.'

She must have forgotten. The invitation never came.

On the long journey home, I suddenly started to cry.

'If you were a girl who could open her mouth and make herself pleasant to people,' said my mother with the spite she showed when disappointed, 'you might have got something.'

When Andrew heard the story, he glinted at me through his fever with a friendly malice.

'I didn't want anything,' I said.

'She's a silly girl, isn't she, Mummy? She'll never be rich.'

'I don't want to be rich.' I was relieved that at last I was revealed to myself.

'You don't want to make money for your mother?' My mother turned from me and ran her fingers through Andrew's fine, pale hair. 'But my little boy will. He'll look after his mother, won't he?'

She smiled at him: he smiled back, and their understanding of each other made me feel excluded and afraid.

London, 1939.

In A Winter Landscape

In A Winter Landscape

(To Prince Antoine Bibesco)

Everyone who went there to ski for the first time took a photograph of the train. It had a little black engine with a tall funnel that bulged like an onion at the top. We thought it must date back to the '60s or the '70s, but on the side was written 'Munich, 1910'. It looked like a little muscular pony. Behind was an open truck for the wood. Behind that was the carriage, yellow-varnished, a platform back and front, big windows and long seats, like an old-fashioned tram-car. In this the hotel guests travelled. Last of all came a closed-in truck for the skis, luggage and any peasant who wanted to go from one halt to another in the valley. The truck had a coat of blue paint, weathered now so it looked like verdigris.

In the carriage the windows were sealed against the cold. The backsides of the respectable guests were packed like fruits in transit. The women wore hats copied from copies of the French, decorated coats, gloves, high-heeled shoes; the men wore their best city clothes. When they arrived they would dress correctly for 'the sport' – but until arrival no unconventionality could be tolerated. There were some children – little fur coats, muffs on strings, velvet bonnets, white bootees – who whimpered and gazed at the foreigners with round, unfriendly eyes. The hotel was a family hotel. Everyone was going there for Christmas.

As the journey was to last from early morning until supper-time, each family had brought a bag packed with rolls and salami and Thermos flasks. Immediately the engine gave its first jerk forward the rolls were split in half, filled with salami and handed out to the children. The children peeled off the salami-rind and dropped it on the floor. We were standing up, so they were able to wipe their fingers on our ski-trousers.

When we opened the door for air, someone slammed it indignantly shut: but that did not keep out the cold. It merely kept in the smell of garlic and sweat. At the first halt we left the carriage and went into the truck with the skis. On the return journey, we went all the way with the skis.

At the beginning of the long, slow climb up to the hotel, the valley lay about us coloured by sparse damp, winter grass. As we rose, we came into the snow region, but the snow was old. It was glassy and sinister in the grey light. We passed a little waterfall frozen into a glass waterfall. We felt, if we could get out and look, we would find dust on it.

It was dark when we reached the hotel. The snow was no better here and experienced skiers began grumbling at once, but next day there was a heavy fall. After that it snowed almost every day for a week. The new snow fell in grains like fluffy seeds. It settled in grains on the old snow and drifted about there with swansdown gentleness. The old snow had been white enough, but the new was whiter. It was like white light. We could not make it into balls. If we scooped it up and squeezed it, it just fell into powder again as soon as we opened our hands. When it froze hard it squeaked under our feet as we walked and had the dry, tight feel of boracic powder.

The mornings were beautiful. The snow flanked the paths in long, unbroken curves. We could put our hands into it and sift it about like sand and then shake every grain off our fingers. Up in the pine forests the trees were like sugar trees. After a while all this whiteness hurt the eyes and it became scarcely possible to see anything. Between the grizzled pines flashed the splinters of the low sun and above was the pure enamel blue of the sky.

Near the hotel was a little lake with a tea-house built out into the water for summer visitors. The tea-house was a shabby red, but now, outlined and glittering with frost, it had a Japanese look. The snow had been swept from the ice and a loudspeaker broadcast dance music; a few skaters pressed forward and turned and lifted feet to the rhythm of the music. People stood and watched them. Most kept cautiously to going forward; but one or two were good and conscious of their audience. These had all the attention they could want. Two young men in wind-jackets excelled everyone. They joined hands and swept forward to the music, their bodies leaning out like figureheads, their feet a little behind but following beautifully, knowing exactly what must be done and doing it exactly: now the right foot forward, now the left, now the right leg lifted and a swing round, arm in arm, a beautifully clean turn on one foot and away again in another direction to lift feet and change arms and cross and recross one another, all in time to the music and so smoothly. Their coarse faces expressed the nothingness of complete satisfaction.

Jake said: 'They're too conceited even to look pleased with themselves.'

Watching them for some reason made us feel sad and we thought that here we were in the centre of Europe with the enemy between us and our own country. We thought when we were refugees, perhaps we would look back on these as the happiest days of our lives.

The afternoons clouded over. It was dark by four o'clock.

People began to leave the skiing slopes early, for wolves sometimes approached the hotel. If anyone lingered, they would see the figures of the others wavering and dwindling into the frightening twilight. Sometimes, while it was still light, a mist would come down through the pines and cut off everything. There was nothing to do but return to the hotel with its matchboarded walls and home-made electric light. The outdoor cold after sunset hurt one's whole body. The stream, too swift to freeze, steamed against the air. We hurried for relief to the heavy, oil-smelling, headache-heat of the hotel radiators.

The sun had not risen when we left. The air was grey. It was almost as cold as night. We knew what to do. There was an iron stove in one corner of the truck. We took two or three armfuls of logs from the tender-truck into the luggage-truck and made a fire in the stove. The passengers in the carriage watched out at us with amazement.

The damp logs, green fungus on the bark, smoked and perfumed the air. It was soon warm enough in the truck for comfort. There were two small windows without glass. We could kneel on the luggage and look out at the valley and feel the frozen air stream past our faces. As we descended, the snow lay thinner and we could see bushes and the hair-fine branches of the trees. A pewter and glass landscape repeated itself against a pewter sky. In places young trees covered the hills. The snow had blown from them, but lay thickly on the ground so the sloping hillsides were outlined through the smoke-fine fringing of trees. The hills rose and fell, rose and fell, drawn in white against the dark sky, detailed over with amazing delicacy by trees, houses and frozen rivers.

The houses were one-roomed, their windows boarded against the cold or hung with cloth. Each was topped by a straw roof like a peaked cap four times as high as itself. There was no telling barns and byres from dwelling-houses. They were all built the same and boarded up and extinguished by their tall, straw roofs. A few peasants followed the paths between the fields. They walked in single file – the men first in tight trousers and short coats of whitish frieze and sheepskin caps shaped like the roofs; the women followed in embroidered sheepskin jackets and red skirts. They turned their serious faces as we went past, but barely looked at us.

The river followed the train line. The ice, melting in parts, varied from white to a pale, icy green. Sometimes it was smashed to uncover the green-black waters below.

We stopped for five minutes at a half-way halt. There was a steady whine in the air. We got out to look. We had stopped beside a sawmill. There was an open fronted shed with a circular saw spinning round in the middle and enough logs stacked around to last a lifetime. The saw was cutting more logs. It could have cut four times as many a minute if the peasants had moved more quickly, but they saw no need to hurry. One of them held the wood to the saw, in an instant the steel slid through the wood, then he slowly pushed the pieces aside. The other peasant as slowly picked them up and stacked them – and all the time the saw whirred away with furious energy.

There were two stoves to heat the shed. We stood beside them and watched. One peasant looked at us with serious, disinterested, winter-bitten face, then went on slowly and disinterestedly feeding the saw. The other one kept his back to us.

Another man in a heavy overcoat, fur cap and jack-boots, was watching the saw. We knew he had not come from the carriage, which had remained sealed, its windows blurred, the faces showing through like tuberous plants in a conservatory. We supposed him to be a rich peasant, the owner of the sawmill, perhaps, or even of a small estate. He took no notice of us.

It was nearly noon. The day as light as it was likely to be, and still too cold to permit one to stand for more than a few minutes. Jake and David filled their arms with logs again and we went back to our truck. We stoked up the stove and sat round it on the suitcases. The brittle, white-pewter light struck upwards from the snow to the roof of the truck. The singing of the saw went on like a noise in nature. The stove burnt up a log in a few minutes. Its iron glowed rose-red, yet only thawed a few feet of the air about it.

The train gave a grunt. As it moved off someone jumped on to the platform of the truck and pushed open the door. In came the man in jack-boots. It was evident he had expected to have the truck to himself. He frowned at seeing us sitting round the stove and half-turned away. He would have sat by himself in some corner if he could, but there was nowhere to sit. David made room for him at once. He stood for a while then sat down in a withdrawn, resentful way.

We knew he could not be a Rumanian. It was only the first year of the war. A crowd of Rumanians, each drawing confidence from the others, might show resentment of our freedom, but one alone would be nervous, ingratiating, eager to assure us that the English had every right to think themselves a great people. If he were a Hungarian – and here we were almost on the frontier – he would surely be a more charming person!

This man had a sullen self-possession. Even David had nothing to say to him. Although he sat so close to us that he was pressing against Jake's arm, we three felt we sat together and apart from him and waited like an audience for him to speak.

He was a tall man, thin and bony, with a pallid, hard-boned

face. He had a thin, down-drooping mouth like Dante's, but only his fixed expression of morose self-satisfaction – the expression of one who hopes his presence is causing discomfort – distinguished his face. His shineless leather boots sprawled surprisingly long and narrow in front of him.

He said suddenly in French: 'You're American, aren't you?'

'English,' David introduced himself: 'David Bailey: and this is my wife and this is Jake Jackson. We come from Bucharest.'

'I'm going there,' said the man without looking at us. He was beginning to feel the heat from the stove. He edged an inch or two from it and at last had to undo his overcoat. It fell open and we saw beneath it a greyish uniform with grey metal buttons. We knew at once he was a Polish soldier. We had seen hundreds like him coming in lorries to Bucharest. The lorries, riddled with shrapnel-holes and coated with mud, had swayed from side to side of the road, their drivers half-asleep at the wheel. The officers and civilians had come in cars. They parked anywhere. They just came to a stop. One could see them with the windscreens blotted out with mud, mattresses tied to the roofs, the people inside sprawling open-mouthed, asleep, their exhaustion overcoming for a while cold and hunger. The civilians who had money – and the wealthier ones brought bags of sovereigns, napoleons and golden dollars privately minted in Austria – took the Simplon at once for Paris. English money, and Englishmen to administer it, arrived in Bucharest to care for the rest. The soldiers were interned.

As soon as these refugees ceased to seem pitiable, stories began to circulate about their ingratitude and vanity and foolish, self-centred pride. Those who had lent them rooms or houses found their guests had settled in for good. In a few weeks everyone was bored with them and even ready to blame them for starting the war.

'What are you doing in Rumania?' asked the Pole.

'We work here,' said Jake.

'When our country was invaded,' said the Pole, 'every man who was abroad hurried back to defend her.'

'We were ordered to stay here,' said Jake. The Pole stared sullenly at the stove.

'They have more men in England than they can train,' David explained. 'We wanted to return, but we were told to stay here.'

'You should have been trained in readiness,' said the Pole. 'You should have been prepared to defend Poland.'

'We couldn't do more than we did,' said Jake sharply. 'And what about Poland being trained in readiness. Isn't it true you tried to fight the German tanks on horseback?'

'We have our traditions,' said the Pole. 'Poland suffered alone. She fought unaided. Now we will see how long the others fight.'

'They're all fighting for Poland,' said David.

'Nonsense,' said the Pole sourly, 'they're fighting for themselves.'

After that there was a long silence. At last I asked him what he was doing in this part of the country. He did not look at me, but answered: 'A few of us got down to Transylvania and were interned. We heard they were letting them escape from the bigger camps, but there were too few of us for anyone to bother. Nobody thought we would try to escape because we were too well off where we were. We had nothing to do. We'd lie on our bunks all day and think of Poland. Suddenly, last night, I knew I had had enough of it – and I knew I could get away. Why should these Rumanians care? They confiscated all the gold we brought from the banks and now they have to feed us – better for them if we go. I put a towel round me and crawled across the snow and under the wire. I spent the night walking east and this morning I came on this railway. I knew it must lead to the main line.'

'Have you had anything to eat?' asked David.

'I got bread and *juica* from a cottage.'

'You have some money?'

'No. Everything we had was taken from us at the camp.'

'Then how will you get to Bucharest?' asked Jake.

'I'll walk. I'll follow the line.'

'It will take you a month.'

'I have plenty of time.'

We settled down again into silence. The Pole interrupted. 'The war hasn't started for you yet' he said. 'You do not think perhaps you will be refugees one day.' We did not answer and he said nothing more.

We came at last to the main-line halt. The carriage emptied itself in a squealing struggle to obtain one of the half-dozen peasants who acted as porters. While we were carrying our skis and bags across the line to the platform, we forgot the Pole. When we looked round, we saw he had followed us. He caught David's eye and, jumping down on to the line, he started walking determinedly eastwards. David shouted to him. He looked round.

'Don't go yet,' said David.

Without question or surprise, the Pole climbed back to the platform and waited.

David said in English to Jake. 'We'll have to get this fellow a ticket. He can't walk to Bucharest.'

'I don't see why not. He's got nothing else to do.'

'He'd freeze at night, or be eaten by wolves.'

'He doesn't seem the sort to freeze.'

'Don't be a fool, Jake; you know we'll have to get him a ticket.'

'And he knows it, too.'

'That makes no difference.'

'Oh, damn the Poles! They're everywhere.'

I followed David and Jake over to the waiting-room. It was crowded. Everyone had huddled there away from the wind. At the end was the ticket-office with its wooden shutter down and people rapping on the shutter, and shouting and making irritable Balkan gestures. Placed against the walls and on ledges and darkening the small, grimy windows, were plants in pots, all very dim and dry and dusty and shrunken with cold. The ticket-office shutter shot up suddenly and a red face above a dark uniform began shouting back at the travellers. David kept sending me outside to make sure the Pole had not run off. He remained where we had left him. Some twenty minutes later we got our tickets. David was afraid now that the Pole would not accept his, but he took it without comment.

I became angry then, but David said: 'What does it matter? We didn't do it for gratitude.'

The train, when it arrived, was crowded. Every train now was crowded. The whole country was under arms awaiting attack. The soldiers, who had to pay their own fares, travelled about the country in passenger trains. There were not many trains. All, even the 'expresses', stopped at every station and the peasants got on and off continually. Every journey was a long journey in time, if not in space.

Seven officers lay fast asleep in one carriage with their faces pressed against the bald, grimy plush and dirty curtains. David persuaded them to move so there was room for me, but he and Jake had to stand. The Pole disappeared.

The damp in the air had covered the carriage windows with

long ferns of frost. One could scrape off the frost and see through the glass the white landscape going past. This was wheat-growing country, treeless, the fields repeating themselves in hills and hollows that looked barren, as though made of salt.

The peasants were packed in the corridors. Some lay on the floor. Some were prepared to stand for the full twenty hours of the journey to Bucharest. A girl in a wide red skirt sat on the handle of a basket. When she moved I could see beneath an embroidered linen covering, two geese in the basket. They were very big, very white, silent, dignified, but sick of being trodden on.

As we made our way along to the restaurant-car we looked for the Pole, but could not see him anywhere. When we reached the car, there he was lunching with a little dark man, who looked uncomfortable and annoyed. He gave us a gloomy stare and turned his face away, as though we had ill-treated him. This amused Jake, who watched the two of them until the little man paid the bill and they passed us and went out. Neither of them had spoken during their meal. The Pole ignored us. We had decided to spend the night at Sighişoara, so we hoped to see no more of him.

But, when, at Sighişoara, we had got our luggage through the carriage window and fought our way out to join it, we found the Pole standing on the platform beside us.

He accused us: 'You are getting out here?'

'Yes, we're spending the night here.'

'And when does this train get to Bucharest?'

'Tomorrow morning.'

'I'll stay here too,' he said.

'Not with us,' said Jake, but he spoke in English. He hoisted his rucksack on to his shoulder and walked off.

David, following, sighed. He was always hoping circumstances would let him evade responsibility, but they never did.

With an air of obstinate peevishness, the Pole followed us. The waiting-room behind the platform was crowded with peasants eating from their bundles.

It was twilight. The air outside was a bright, frigid blue. The snow on the roofs was blue. The silhouette of the town with its towers and churches mounting the hillside, stood out in a plum-bloom blue against the frost-bitten blue of the sky.

We wanted a taxi because of the cold, but there were only sleighs. These were painted blue to match the town. They were small and close to the ground, with dirty straw on the floor, but their horses, unlike the wretched Bucharest horses, were plump under their woolly winter hair.

We got into a sleigh – David and I on one seat; Jake on the other. Jake put his rucksack on the fourth seat and smirked at the Pole, who was watching us. David lifted it down and said: 'Come on. There's room for you.'

Off we went with a jingle of bells through the blue streets with the air singing past our ears. Our faces became frozen so we could not feel them at all, but our ears hurt all the time.

We crossed a river. Blue snow lay on the ice. We could see the frosted branches of the weeping willows overhanging the invisible waters. The houses were dark but occasionally a little shop threw a glimmer of light on to the lumpy, dirty snow caked on the pavements. The hotel was surprisingly big. It looked like a barracks. When the sleigh stopped before it the driver, his frieze trousers fitting his legs like breeches, his jacket short and trimmed with fur, tumbled off the seat. 'Drunk,' said Jake, clicking his tongue. The driver picked himself up gaily and swayed with our bags into the hotel.

Inside was bare and new. David took three rooms – one was for the Pole, who accepted his key as he had his ticket – and we went upstairs to wash. The bedroom with its fumed oak and its golden satin eiderdown surprised us. Someone told us later that a lot of families from Bucharest spent the heat of the summer up here in the hills.

The Pole was waiting for us when we went downstairs and followed us out for supper. The hotel was in the main street. The shops were closed now. The whole place looked as though it were shuttered in against the cold. We felt the frozen snow like glass through our shoes. Snow was heaped in the gutters. The road was covered with snow that had been hardened flat by sleighs and looked like felt. We saw one or two private cars, probably belonging to factory owners, but everything else moved on sleighs.

Jake had been here before and knew where the restaurant was. It looked like a small shop and seemed as shuttered and dark as the rest of the street, but the door opened when we pushed it and inside we saw a counter for the sale of sausages, cheese, olives, pickles and *ţuica*. At one end of the counter, done in miniature but in the best traditions of old Rumanian restaurants, there was a display of the food on the menu: steak, garlic sausages, chicken and frankfurters. We were hungry.

The inner room was the restaurant. There were half a dozen tables covered with white paper and a couple of gipsies who started to play a modern dance tune as soon as we entered. At one table was a crowd of boys, friends of the waiter, who stopped talking and stared as soon as they saw us. We were not only visitors, we were foreigners – that must have been more than anyone hoped for in the middle of winter in Sighişoara.

We took the table farthest from the music before we realized it was also farthest from the stove. We sat with our coats on and ate grilled steak and drank *ţuica* that had been heated with sugar and pepper. The *ţuica* was very good. We ordered another half-litre and then another.

As we drank, the Pole, slowly and with the cumbersome movement of a tortoise wakening from age-long sleep, unbuttoned his coat and began to come to life. We had forgotten him. Jake and David had lapsed into English and were talking about the war. The Pole made a few slight hiccuping noises, then he joined in the conversation, which he did not understand, by giving an occasional '*Oui, oui*', and '*Non, non*'. When they were reminded of him, Jake and David started speaking again in French that he might not be excluded. As soon as he could understand what they were saying, he settled back again into gloomy silence. Then, suddenly, he shouted aloud: 'Poland has not perished yet.'

The town lads, who had lost interest in us by now, sat up and listened. The musicians paused in order to miss nothing. The Pole, with a look that showed he was aware of the expectancy, shut his mouth. When it was evident that nothing more was to be got out of him, everyone returned to his occupation, and the Pole gazed round, grieved, and after a pause, started mumbling: 'I remember when I worked in Lwow . . .' When no one took any notice, he repeated it more and more loudly until David and Jake broke off and looked at him. Then he drank a cup of *ţuica* slowly, swallowed slowly, and said impressively: 'I remember when I worked in Lwow . . .'

'Yes?' encouraged David.

'Ah!' said the Pole and stared gloomily into his empty cup.

None of us was very sober by now. The Pole had begun to seem a joke.

'Come on, cheer up!' shouted Jake, slapping him on the back. At first he did not seem to mind, then, as though he realized he ought to mind, he sat upright, his nostrils distended, his eyes starting, and said fiercely: 'How dare you! How dare you touch me! You, who did not fight for Poland!'

'Oh, shut up!' said Jake.

'Have some more *ţuica* and forget about Poland,' David said.

'I don't want any more *ţuica*,' said the Pole, but he let David fill his cup, 'and I shall never forget about Poland. Never.' He sipped meditatively: 'I remember when I was in Lwow . . .'

We did not interrupt. There was a long pause and at last he went on grudgingly, as though it were impossible now not to go on: 'I was in love with a girl. In the evenings we used to walk round the streets together and talk. Nothing else – but we had plenty to talk about. I told her everything. I thought she told me everything.'

He emptied his cup and refilled it. Another pause. He continued, not so grudgingly now, overlooking the injury for a time: 'I can remember we often went down a road by the canal. I can remember hearing some dogs barking, answering one another, somewhere behind the houses. It was dark. The roads were only half-lighted . . . and it all meant something. Yes, it meant something, but I don't know what. It seemed to me that I'd discovered something. Everything was important to me in those days.' He paused for so long now that David and Jake started talking again. At once the Pole interrupted them sternly: 'But nothing here is important. This place means nothing. You mean nothing. Your faces mean nothing.'

'Never mind,' said Jake.

David asked: 'Did you marry her?'

The Pole stared down darkly. 'No,' he replied, at last, 'I saved every penny to marry her, then one day she told me she was engaged to someone else. I'd kept her waiting too long. I didn't even know she knew another man. They got married and went to live in Warsaw. I used to get sent there sometimes and I always visited them. When the war started she was going to have a baby. Her husband was killed. She's probably still in Warsaw.'

'And you're trying to get back to her?' I asked.

'No,' the Pole looked surprised, 'I'm trying to get to France. I can fight for Poland there.'

'Poland is important?' asked Jake.

The Pole stared at him in silence. Jake, flushing slightly, gave a laugh, then called loudly for the bill.

When we got back to the hotel, the Pole walked straight upstairs to his room. He had not spoken again. We hoped he would catch the first train in the morning and when we awoke, we dressed slowly to give him time to get away. But we got down to the hotel café to find him sitting there reading a German newspaper mounted on a cane holder. His first words were: 'Everyone here speaks German.'

David explained: 'This is a Saxon town – the people are practically German. You know the Pied Piper legend? Well, these people are supposed to be descended from the children who disappeared.'

The Pole broke in as though he had been waiting for a chance to make a complaint: 'You shouldn't have brought me here.'

'No, I suppose we shouldn't,' said Jake. The Pole gave an irritated gesture and returned to his paper. We got Rumanian papers from the rack and ordered coffee and rolls for four.

Both the outer and inner windows were heavily frosted, but we could tell by the colour of the light that the sun was shining. As more people came into the café and the room warmed, the glass cleared in patches and we could look out at tiny pictures of the distant Gothic buildings climbing up the hillside. Against the delicate blue sky, with its stippling of green overhead, the snow-silvered glimpses of churches and towers were like pictures painted on china. We wanted to go out at once. The next train was not until one o'clock. We left the Pole to do what he pleased about it and, of course, he followed.

The light in the street was very bright. It was a New Year holiday and the shops were shut. The town seemed deserted. An occasional sleigh whipped past in a jingle of bells, but we passed no one on the pavements. We came to the main square. Here a solitary small boy was tobogganing down a slope and scattering as he went a multitude of pigeons. We took a path up between the roofs to the hilltop. When we got up a little way we looked back and saw the roofs below us like folded slips of white velvet. Each chimney held up its collar of snow. A smoke gauze lay over the frigid glitter of the snow. As the path grew steeper it turned into steps beside which the sedate houses rose one above the other, painted terracotta, pink, lime-green, grey-blue, orange or cocoa-brown. Everywhere the snow, unbroken and brilliant on roofs and ledges, heightened the colours.

The lower steps had been cleared, but as we rose higher we had to feel for foot-hold. The way was diverted at times under Gothic arches, corbelled, painted and gilded, that framed the bright corners of houses and the blinding glitter of light on snow. Suddenly we came to the top of the steps and saw the church – a dull piece of modern Gothic, but with ancient, very tall, black tombstones rising from snow behind an intricately-wrought railing. Whenever we paused, the Pole paused, too, but when we looked at him he stared blankly over our heads.

'Don't you think it's rather a pleasant town?' David asked him.

He shrugged his shoulders.

'We're just wasting his time,' said Jake.

We started up a new set of steps to the hilltop. As we rose

from the protecting buildings, the air got colder and colder. It was almost impossible to breathe for cold. It tricked out everything with diamond-edged acuteness. The colours were bitten in with cold. It made us almost weep for our hands and nose and feet, but it also took away every haze of reflection that might dull the brain.

We were now walking up through public gardens. A large building stood at the top.

'What is it?' asked Jake. 'It's a school. The Rumanians would have put the Prefectura up there.'

'The French would have put the church,' said David.

'And we would have put a public monument – but we would have cleared the steps for appearances' sake.'

The school was closed for the holidays. Fall after fall of snow had blotted out the gardens, so one could not tell where there were paths and where grass or steps. Once or twice we sank down to our knees, or stepped on something unexpectedly hard and lost balance. The Pole tripped on a rail and came to his knees with a thud. He shouted out angrily in Polish. We laughed at him as he brushed himself down, but he did not laugh.

The summit, just behind the school, was a small, square garden with paths indenting the snow. Here, between the frost-tipped branches of the trees, we could survey the whole town running down the sides of the hill and crowded in a hollow round the central square. We could see the rapid horse-sleighs passing smoothly over the roads and the big, slow sleighs, loaded with wood, and drawn by heavy, fawn-coloured oxen. While we watched, the pigeons rose like a handful of seed flung into the air. They took three turns, flashing from iron-grey to white, then poured down like seed through a funnel to settle in a bunch on the road.

We could look out to the surrounding hills and see through

the snow the division of fields, the ridges for vines or hops, the poles, the black rows of fruit trees and the isolated farms.

In the valley running between the hills were factory chimneys from which a red smoke rolled out to colour the sky so it looked like the sky in childhood pictures of biblical destruction.

From the other side of the garden, over a wall ribbed with wind-driven snow, we could see into a modern cemetery. Gravestones overhung gravestones, hundreds of them dropping acutely down and down out of sight.

'All so ugly,' I said. 'There were only a few of the old stones – but now there are too many people and one feels affronted by the sight of so much death,' and I returned to where the valley ran white into the distance. On either side the steep flanks of the hills were cultivated in terraces that hung there like the gardens of Babylon.

The Pole broke in on our conversation: 'We're late for the train.'

David looked at his watch. 'We haven't much time,' he agreed, 'but we haven't got to catch it. We're not due back until Monday.'

'Let us stay one more night,' I said.

The Pole interrupted irritably: 'There is no time to waste in talking.'

David said: 'We have decided to stay another day.'

'But I do not wish to stay.'

Jake said: 'If you hurry back, you'll catch the train. You can go straight to the station.'

'Don't worry about the hotel bill,' said David.

The Pole stared at us as though some inexcusable trick had been played on him, but we stood our ground remorselessly. After a moment he glanced down to the town, then swung round and away across the snow.

[103]

Suddenly David ran after him. Jake and I followed without enthusiasm. David overtook him and when we came up, was asking him: 'What are you going to do in Bucharest? I mean, for money?'

The Pole looked contemptuously from one to the other of us: 'I shall manage very well,' he said. 'All the buttons on my uniform are made of gold.'

We stared unbelievingly at the grey metal buttons.

'They're leaded over,' he said, 'I had them made two years ago.' His mouth dropped down further in a bitter smirk. 'You see, we were not unprepared.'

We had nothing to say. We watched him stride off.

'Damn him!' said Jake when the Pole was out of sight, 'how did he manage to put us in the wrong?'

'After all we did for him!' I said.

'What did we do for him?' asked David, giving me a push. 'We spent some money we could well afford.'

'What did he want?' asked Jake angrily. 'What did he expect from us?'

I said: 'He expected something. He followed us; he told us about the girl. He thought we had something to give.'

We all stood looking down where the Pole had gone. 'Well, it's too late now,' said Jake at last, 'and we're only worrying because it's too late. So let's be thankful we can go and eat in peace.'

We never saw the Pole again.

Cairo, 1941.

A Spot of Leave

A Spot of Leave

A Spot of Leave

At five o'clock, when the afternoon was deepening into violet-scented, spring twilight, Phillips and Aphrodite met for tea at Larides'. This was the hour when the Alexandrine Greeks drank coffee. Sometimes men dropping into the café from offices and women pausing in their shopping, would stand at the counter and eat with a silver, two-pronged fork, a couple of cakes. The counter displayed immense chocolate boxes tied with ribbons. The cakes were rich and elaborate: sponge-cake, macaroon or feather-fine pastry laden with cream, strawberries, chocolate, icing, nuts, preserved fruits, rich jams or chestnut paste. They were displayed behind glass.

'And the ladies,' thought Phillips in his captain's uniform, his young face decorated with a cavalry moustache he would have shrunk from wearing when a civilian clerk, 'the ladies are like the cakes.'

They came and went in the shop, charming in their flowered silks, their furs, their confectionery hats, their sheer silk stockings from the United States and their delicate shoes. Each whose husband was of the necessary income-level wore like a trophy on her ring finger a diamond of at least two carats. All were completed with flowers and perfumes, as though a fashionable wedding might be sprung on them at any moment. Phillips, staring at them with his slightly bulging, stone-blue eyes, nodded agreement with himself: 'Just like the cakes – and I wouldn't mind a bite.'

'It is shocking, don't you think, such a display?' said Aphrodite.

'Shocking?' Phillips turned to her and laughed. 'Far from it.'

'But in Palestine you lack sugar.'

'Well, the civilians are a bit short.'

'Here they have too much, yet they refuse to export. In this window last week there was a wedding cake – eight cakes on top of one another, white with sugar. And in Palestine children are ill for need of it.'

'Too bad,' agreed Phillips, looking back into the shop's bustle and fluffing up his moustache with his hand as dark eyes glanced towards him. He had admired Aphrodite's English every time he had been at a loss for something to say, but his ear was more intrigued by the chirruping, inaccurate French of the ladies who moved among the bows on the chocolate-boxes like flowers among butterflies. The men were as elegant. Phillips noticed one – small, elderly, plump, exquisite in silver-grey with pointed shoes – who followed a shop-girl and supervised her packing of a satin-covered box. He moved like a bright insect through the garden of sweets and women, pausing his long, quivering, forefinger over the trays of fondants, darting it like a sting when he made his choice, then rejecting and choosing again, making, unmaking and re-making his mind with agitation.

'Wonder who the old boy's buying those for!' said Phillips.

'For himself.'

'Surely not.'

'Yes.' Aphrodite gave a decided shake of her head. 'He is a

relative of mine. He is very rich. He always buys himself a box when he makes money on the Bourse. Every day he makes more money except when it looks as though the war might end soon, then the Bourse is frightened.'

'Really!' After some reflection Phillips said: 'You have a lot of relatives.'

'Everyone has a lot of relatives,' said Aphrodite.

Beyond the giant window-bottles filled with crystallized fruits, violets and angelica, went a stream of people: smart Greeks, rich Egyptians, some wearing the fez, servants in galabiahs, French sailors with red pom-poms on their hats and every sort of English and Allied serviceman.

Some French officers, from the pale-grey battleships that had lain motionless in Alexandria harbour since the fall of France, sat at the near-by table. They drank coffee like the Greeks. They, thought Aphrodite, had become at home here because they had adapted themselves at once. The English tried to make a place adapt itself to them. Phillips, for instance, had settled into his basket-chair and without consulting her had at once ordered tea. He had got it just as he had wanted it – hot and strong with milk and sugar. Larides' had learnt to serve it that way the day the first Englishman explained his needs. The Wrens, ATS and nurses, when they arrived, had proved more exacting, for they required the old tea to be emptied out of the pots and fresh tea put in for each customer – but, they, too, got what they wanted. They sat round the tables with the confident look of the girls she had seen in teashops when she went to stay with her husband's family at Littlehampton.

'You like the tea here?' she asked Phillips.

'Just the job,' he answered. 'Laid on as mother made it.'

'Your nurses,' said Aphrodite, watching the table opposite, 'they do not approve of us, do they? They have seen men dying and they think here are all these people who only make money out of the war.'

'They're jealous,' declared Phillips. 'They know you've got nice silk stockings and they've only got cotton ones. You have got nice silk stockings, haven't you?' he gazed humorously under the table. 'That's what we like to see when we get a spot of leave.'

'Don't women wear silk stockings in Jerusalem?'

'Well, yes, they do if they can get them – but I used to be up in the blue, you know. I can remember what a treat it was to see you girls nicely dressed. And it's still a treat. I'm glad your husband doesn't take too dim a shufti of me trotting you round a bit.'

'Why should he?' asked Aphrodite. 'He's an Englishman.'

'Even an Englishman can be jealous.'

'We are modern,' said Aphrodite, as though the suggestion of jealousy were an insult. She thought back to a few years before when, unmarried, she had the reputation of being the most 'modern' girl in Alexandria. Indeed, so 'modern' had her behaviour been that it had led to endless rows at home and her mother had said: 'You will never get a husband now. There is not a Greek of good family who would have you.' 'Then I'll marry an Englishman,' she said, and she did.

'My parents did not like me to marry James. He was only a clerk in the English bank – but I loved him. I love Englishmen. They are so intelligent, such breadth of mind, so "modern" – the Greeks are like Orientals. In England women are free.'

'Well, I suppose they are,' Phillips agreed without enthusiasm. 'But nice girls aren't too free.'

'My parents wanted me to marry a rich cotton-merchant. An old man who was always drunk. A Copt, too! Think of it. "You can reform him," my mother said, but I said: "Why should I? If he wants to be drunk all the time, it is of no interest to me." Then James was sent to work in Cairo and they were glad. I said nothing. I pretended I had forgotten him. Then one day I started to cry with a toothache. "What I suffer," I said. "Oh, what I suffer!" They were alarmed and said I must go to our dentist in Cairo. So I went and he made an X-ray of my teeth and one had twisted roots. "Look, mother," I said, "look at my insides – how terrible!" So they agreed I should go to stay with my aunt in Cairo and have my teeth mended. When I was two days in Cairo I got married to James.'

'Good Lord!' commented Phillips. 'What did the pater say?'

'You mean my father? He said much, but in the end it is all right. He is a banker. He used influence and James was brought back here to a position.'

'O.K. for James, eh?'

'We are very happy.'

'Oh, are you!' Phillips showed a twinge of annoyance that made Aphrodite smile.

She was reminded of the days before her happy marriage when she had roused endless twinges of jealousy in the young men of Alexandria. Now, after two years of contentment with James, she felt afresh the glow of the chase. In a moment the situation, which she had scarcely grasped before, fell into position and she saw herself in control. Looking upon Phillips as her natural victim, Aphrodite's eyes and colour grew brighter and her whole manner eased into an indolent charm. 'Tell me about your home in England,' she said, as she pushed back her teacup and lit a cigarette.

'Oh!' Phillips was disconcerted for a moment, but he was not unprepared. Ever since he had got through the OCTU and his office experience had led him to a job in Pal Base, he had been readjusting his background.

Aphrodite, watching him as she listened to him, saw him quite newly as rather handsome in his youthful, blue-eyed fairness. His moustache hid his worst feature, his small, prim mouth. She began to build up from what was attractive in him, the elements of romance. She knew exactly how it should continue from here and she would let it continue. She listened with all the necessary smiling interest, the glow, the flattering absorption in him that was to be his undoing. When Phillips, looking up into her fixed dark glance, blushed slightly, she thought: 'He is sweet, and only a boy.'

'What is your mother like?' she asked, keeping him talking.

'Rather handsome, the mater. Dresses awfully well, but a bit severe with the poor old pater. Plays golf, too.' He added this last touch, which he had not thought of before, and the picture came into focus.

'Have you a photograph of her?' asked Aphrodite.

'Yes – at least, I mean, no. Not with me,' Phillips blushed again.

After a smiling pause Aphrodite said: 'Tonight my husband is going out for a business meeting. Come in and have a drink and keep me company.'

' 'Fraid I can't. I've got a date with another fellow on leave from my office.'

She looked surprised rather than hurt, but smiled: 'I hope you're not going to Maisie's House.'

He gave her a startled stare. There was a long silence before he suggested they should meet next day for tea.

'Of course,' said Aphrodite. 'And would you like to walk with me along the Corniche?'

'I don't mind,' Phillips's manner was neither eager nor indifferent. Aphrodite could interpret his manner as she wished.

When he had seen her to a taxi, he called one for himself and started back to his hotel by the sea. Settled into his corner, watching out at the brilliance of the street in that moment before darkness and the blackout fell, he contemplated his life now lived in expensive hotels, expensive restaurants, taking tea with the daughters of wealthy bankers, jumping into taxis ... and he murmured to himself in the almost forgotten argot of the desert: 'Bit of all right, eh, chum?'

Aphrodite's flat in the Sharia Cherif Pasha was as English as its basic Frenchness permitted. Her father had also presented her with a small house at Stanley Bay, where she and James spent the summer. She had, she realized, all she could wish. James had the characteristics she most admired in the English. He was better-looking than Phillips, he was considerate yet met her on an equal footing and showed no resentment of her intelligence. She could not had she wished have found cause for discontent, yet now she felt she was missing an excitement she must find again.

When James came home to supper, she said: 'You know Phillips, the young officer?'

'What about him?'

'You wouldn't mind, would you, if I went to bed with him?'

James did not glance up from his soup as he said: 'I'm tired and I've got to go out to that damned meeting.'

'You wouldn't mind, would you?'

'Mind what?' asked James irritably.

'What I asked – if I slept with Phillips?'

'I don't know,' James kept his glance on his plate. 'I haven't thought about it.'

'But we thought about it a long time ago. We agreed we'd be modern.'

'Then why ask me? You know you can do what you like.'

Aphrodite sighed. She wanted to get these formalities over. Almost she wished now the whole business were over and Phillips safely back in Jerusalem. Yet she was determined to go through with it and in her determination she felt a little drunk, a little lifted above the realities of her everyday life. 'I don't want to deceive you,' she said. 'I want you to be happy about it.'

'All right,' said James. 'I'm happy. Now shut up.'

When he went out, Aphrodite moved restlessly about the flat. She remained in a state of restless inactivity next day until it was time to meet Phillips. James did not speak at breakfast or at luncheon. Phillips, she knew, had only three days more leave and the knowledge filled her with a sense of urgency so that she ached with nervous strain. She ordered the house from habit and she was conscious of James with a worried impatience that was painful to her. What she felt for him was, she knew, intact, but it must remain at a standstill while she lived through this interlude that would prove to her that she was missing nothing.

After luncheon she left the house before James. 'I may not be back for dinner,' she said. He did not reply.

She met Phillips in a café near the old harbour. It was a brilliant spring day and the sea had in it the first green and purple that would deepen with summer. On the other side of the circular harbour was the castle. It stood, on the site of the ancient Pharos, cleanly edged against the sea's colour as though blown bone-white by the wind. The water within the harbour arms sprang up and down.

As they followed the Corniche road with the wind in their faces, Phillips said: 'I've been thinking of having a couple of days in Cairo.'

'You mean, after your leave?'

'No, I'd have to go tomorrow.'

'Alone?' asked Aphrodite.

'Well, the chap from my office is going. I thought of going with him.'

Aphrodite, silent, stared ahead.

'But I don't think I'll go. I like it here.'

'Ah!' Aphrodite smiled. 'Perhaps you do not want to leave me?'

Phillips cleared his throat as though he were doing a comic turn and gave her a coy glance: 'That's about it,' he said.

Conversation became easier after that. On one side of them the concrete houses and blocks of flats stretched far out of sight into the desert. On the other side splashed the mildly choppy sea, its border of rock yellow and porous like rotting cheese.

'It reminds me of Worthing,' said Phillips. 'The only thing is we don't have date palms.'

'I know. I've been to Littlehampton.'

'Good Lord, have you?' and they talked about England and English seaside towns. Aphrodite was gaily critical, while Phillips was nostalgically respectful. They passed Stanley Bay with its closed bathing huts and air of popular entertainment shut up for the winter. The houses still stretched on. In the distance, too far away to be reached, appeared among palms a white-domed palace, the only Oriental thing in sight. They came at last to a thin shelf of rock through which the ancients had cut holes. On a gusty day like this the sea came spouting through them.

'There!' said Aphrodite. 'Isn't that interesting? In the old days people used to fix musical instruments in the holes so the sea could play tunes.'

'Why on earth did they do that?'

'For amusement.'

'Rum idea.'

'But isn't it interesting? I brought you to see it.'

'Did you? Hell of a length this Corniche – as you call it. Better go back now,' and he swung round without waiting for her agreement. Now the wind was behind them, blowing their hair forward. Right at the other end of the great curve of the shore, the main part of the town, growing steely blue as the light failed, was neatly built-up on a bulge of land. A few barrage-balloons were beginning to rise like silver kidneys on threads above the harbour. The wind was growing cold.

'How about a taxi?' said Phillips at Stanley Bay. When they found one and settled inside it, Aphrodite placed herself comfortably against his shoulder. Some minutes passed before he thought to slip an arm round her.

'Now to brew up,' he said with satisfaction.

'What does that mean?'

'Tea, of course. Where shall we go?'

'The same place,' Aphrodite whispered warmly. 'The same table.'

'O.K.,' said Phillips, and: 'We're in luck,' as they entered Larides' and saw their table was free.

When the tea was poured out, when they were pressing their forks through the luscious softness of coffee-cream cakes, Aphrodite felt the moment had come to clarify and speed up the situation. Phillips might have an Englishman's shyness, but he had only three days' more leave.

'I spoke to my husband about you,' she said.

'What did you tell him? Something nice?'

'Of course. I told him I wanted to sleep with you.'

Phillips raised his eyes and fixed them on her. Even then

he had little expression, but he blushed more darkly than he had done for years. 'Good Lord!' he dropped his glance. 'What made you tell him that?'

'Because I didn't want to deceive him. He must know.'

Phillips put a lump of cake into his mouth before he mumbled: 'But there isn't anything for him to know.'

Aphrodite heard because she had been listening: 'You mean you don't want to?'

Phillips swallowed down the last of his cake and pulled himself together. His manner became rather aggressive: 'You ought to know better,' he said. 'A married lady! And you said you were happy.'

'What difference does that make?'

He refused to reply. She drank some tea. There was another pause before she said with a nervous giggle: 'Why don't you want to?'

'Hell, let's drop the subject.' Phillips frowned in indignation and his voice had lost much of its gentility. A hard and edgy silence settled on them. Aphrodite tried once or twice to break it with an anecdote about this person or that passing through the café, but Phillips was unresponsive. When they parted his manner was still cold. He did not suggest their meeting again.

James, supposing Aphrodite would be out, came home late that evening. He found her sitting alone in darkness. As he switched on the light, he said: 'Home early. Did the beautiful romance fall through?'

She did not answer. She was lying back against her chair and sobbing. He stared at her for some moments, then went to her and slid his arm round her. 'What's the matter?' he asked.

She pressed her face against his middle: 'He didn't want me. Now I know I'm getting old.'

'Nonsense,' he said. 'It just showed what a fool he was.'

'No. I know. I know I'm getting old.'

London, 1946.

The Man Who Stole a Tiger

The Man Who Stole a Tiger

The Man Who Stole a Tiger

To me the most extraordinary thing about the whole business was the fact that Tandy was an ex-Borstal boy and, what's more, had actually served a stretch before the war. I don't mean, of course, that as a result he would be less likely to commit the crime – dear me, no! – but that it should be *that* sort of crime! And he was not in prison for theft but for some rather nasty trick like obtaining money by false pretences. Because of that I cannot, with the best will in the world, accept his explanation of why he did it. When he told me his story I said: 'But what made you do all this?'

He rolled up his eyes mournfully and said: 'I just didn't like seeing the poor thing in a cage, Padre.'

In my profession one has to be on guard against the Tandy type – smooth-tongued fellows, always with some sentimental excuse for their less worthy actions. In the services the other men have an apt expression for them that it would ill become me to use.

I do not wish to be uncharitable, but *physically* also Tandy is the kind I distrust – a little man with the sort of white, knobbly face that is said to indicate rickets, a long, pointed nose and a cunning, defensive look that gets my back up. Usually when I go into his cell he is sitting crouched in the corner, his face in his hands. Every time I see him like that,

I'm convinced it is a deliberate pose adopted as soon as he hears my footsteps.

Nevertheless, I've done my best for him. I've questioned him and heard his story through again and again – for, to tell you the truth, there are one or two who think Tandy should be confined in some place other than he is.

When I first met him he was in the German Sanitorium at the top of Mount Scopus. He was one of the survivors of a troopship lost in the Mediterranean. He was picked up suffering from exposure and developed tuberculosis of the lungs. When I took over at Christchurch he had already spent eighteen months in bed with a deflated lung. His case was an obstinate one, I agree, but I could not help wondering – after all, life in a Jerusalem sanitorium was a lot more comfortable than the Western Desert.

I didn't take to him from the first. He was lying on the terrace with half a dozen other lads and, as I came out, I saw his eyes move from my dog's-collar to the packets of cigarettes I'd drawn from the Comforts' Fund and a smirk came over his face. As soon as he saw my eye on him, the smirk disappeared. I know a padre is fair game for such chaps, but if you're like me – a little more intelligent than most, shall I say? – you don't take too kindly to exploitation.

I usually sat for half an hour or so chatting with the lads. If they had any little problems, I was glad to assist. All Tandy ever did was question me about the city outside the hospital. He had arrived on a hospital train at night and been taken straight up to the sanitorium. He had seen nothing of Jerusalem and was very curious about it.

'What's it like, Padre?' he asked me. I couldn't help thinking to myself: Why should you care? For there he was, lying in comfort facing the Valley of the Dead Sea, a golden view that was worth a lifetime's contemplation. I always replied in a general way: 'Well, lads, I hope you'll soon be out to see it for yourselves. And, don't forget, the first thing you must do when you're well enough is come down and have tea at the hostel. It's right inside the old city and I'll conduct you round the holy places myself.'

But when Tandy was allowed out on his own for the first time, he did not come near the hostel. He told me he sat in an olive grove on top of Mount Scopus and gazed down over the old houses enclosed within the walls.

'And what did you think of your first sight of the Holy City?' I asked him.

'Of, lovely, sir,' he said with sly enthusiasm. 'All them domes and things – *very* nice.'

Apparently when he at last ventured down the hill, he followed the main road past the Hebrew University and the Hadassah Hospital, then at some point he branched off and found himself in one of those depressing quarters of the new city that remind one, especially in the hot season, of a Middle West shanty town. Somewhere there he came upon a little zoo. I was unaware there was a zoo in Jerusalem until he told me about it, then I paid it a visit myself. When I went, it was winter, the air was cool and the grass had grown after the autumn rains – but the zoo was a miserable enough little place.

When Tandy came upon it, it was mid-summer and the shabby, flimsy shelters for the beasts stood about like litter on the dry stony earth. There were a number of birds of different sorts and a few small wild animals: foxes, hedge-hogs, gazelles; not much else – but when Tandy went there, there was a tiger.

Tandy, describing the tiger, usually stares at the ground and shuffles his feet and rubs the palm of his right hand over his mouth and chin. I don't know what that conveys – em-barrassment or guilt, perhaps – but he often gets quite eloquent about the tiger. The keeper told him it had come to the zoo as a cub. Now it was almost grown up. It was still in the wooden cage of its babyhood but next door to this a concrete and iron cage was being erected. Meanwhile the young tiger, in all the brilliance of its glistening fur, the beauty of its moving muscles, all that fresh cleanliness that animals have at early maturity, was raging backwards and forwards like a mad thing. The wooden cage shook with its movements. Had it tried, it could easily have broken its way out, but it was unaware there was a way out. It had known no freedom yet it was consumed by the burning memory of ancestral freedom.

Forgive me if I sound rather romantic on the subject of the tiger. Tandy, I must admit, is almost inspiring when he talks of it and I have caught a little of his enthusiasm. He says he felt in the creature's movements, in the golden, glistening vitality of its coat and eyes, its frustrated energy, its rising desires that would remain unfulfilled until they died and the beast itself died of old age in the concrete and iron cage that was being prepared for it. He says he stood there for about an hour watching the exquisite placing of its paws with their sensual perfection of line and colour.

The tiger always took just the same number of steps, backwards and forwards, backwards and forwards, across the cage that was no more than three times the length of its own body. He says he saw it as a doomed creature, a beautiful doomed creature! I can, indeed, imagine it as the glory of that desolate place. I only wish it were still there to give pleasure to all the unfortunate folk who live in those suburbs. I do indeed.

Tandy went back to the zoo half a dozen times, and one day – this is his story and he sticks to it – he determined to 'rescue' the tiger. A curious thing is that just about that time he began to make a most remarkable recovery. He had been neither ill nor well for months; now, suddenly, he seemed another person. At the time, I remember, I put it down to the fact that the war was coming to an end, but it is possible, just possible, that this interest in the tiger had something to do with it.

He says the idea of stealing the creature came into his head one day when he arrived at the zoo to find the new cage complete and the keepers engaged in moving the tiger into it. They connected the two cages by a light wooden bridge covered like a tunnel and left it there until the animal's curiosity lead it to cross to the new cage. Tandy stood and watched the tiger pause in its endless walk and gaze with blank, dispassionate eyes at the black mouth of the bridge. It stared for a moment, then padded again for a few more turns before giving the bridge a second look. This time it went to the mouth of the tunnel, sniffed round it and at last put its front paws on the step as though about to jump in – instead, with one of those movements that are graceful yet weighty and powerful, it swung down again and resumed its walk back and forth.

All the time Tandy says he was trying to will the creature not to go into the new cage.

'But why, my dear fellow?' I said. 'That cage was to be its home.'

'Home!' echoed Tandy darkly, 'prison, you mean. Well, the poor beast went in at last; all innocent like, yet in a way suspicious. And just then, just at that moment, I thought I'd rescue him.'

'Are you sure you mean "rescue", Tandy?' I said, giving a laugh because a show of good-fellowship costs you nothing: 'Sure you don't mean "steal"?'

'What'ud I want to steal a tiger for?' he asked. It was not a question I felt I could answer.

He started there and then making his plans and saving up his pay against the time, still many weeks off, when the rescue could be affected. He began by talking to the keepers, both of whom had got their zoological experience in Vienna. Austrian Jews tend to be the most easy-going of the European Jews in Palestine and Tandy with his smooth, ingratiating manner, got on very well with them. They were willing to answer all Tandy's apparently simple-minded questions about the care and feeding of tigers. He took them gifts of NAAFI goods that were scarce on the civilian market – tinned meats, tea, sugar, soap-flakes – so he was soon welcome whenever he cared to drop into the keepers' hut for tea or coffee. Smoking and talking, he noted where the keys were kept, the habits of the keepers and the fact that on the Jewish Sabbath – from Friday evening until Saturday evening – the zoo was shut, locked and deserted. The Orthodox Jews, who are powerful in Jerusalem, have managed to impose a very strict rule on the city. The patients in the Orthodox Jewish Hospital are not permitted to ring a bell for assistance on the Sabbath, so no doubt the zoo animals, like the sick, could be expected to fend for themselves one day in the week.

Before the war Tandy had been aware of belonging to the criminal minority, but that awareness was broken down in the army where there was almost no privately-owned property and the law was designed to protect not the majority but the minority. Tandy thrived on the attitude of 'Good luck to the chap who can get away with it' and as a practiced criminal he no doubt got away with a good deal before his ailment developed. Now his wits were starting to work again. His next move took him farther into the town: indeed, to the military headquarters inside the King David Hotel. He had heard a rumour that an acquaintance from Cairo called Clark had become a corporal and was working in one of the army offices. Tandy in his 'blues' went and sat on the wall of the King David Hotel until Clark came out for his midday meal.

'Hello, Nobby,' said Tandy.

'Hello, Tan,' said Clark. 'Heard you was a bit under the weather,' and the acquaintance was at once resumed exactly where it had broken off when Tandy left Cairo. The monotony of army life, the boredom, the common complaints about everything, form a basis for intimacy between almost any two men of nearly equal rank. Clark was not very surprised to hear that Tandy wanted to borrow one of those large-scale sectional maps of Egypt you see pinned up on the walls of army offices – 'for a private purpose like'. Clark did not care why Tandy wanted the map. If the 'private purpose' were an illegal one, then good luck to him! Clark was only interested in the fact that Tandy offered, per map, the whole of his week's cigarette issue. As Clark knew the sergeant in charge of the map library he could borrow any map for a reasonable time without risk or trouble, and as a man whose face was known to the military police could get through the barrier with almost any sort of papers under his arm, Clark had no difficulty in getting the maps out to Tandy. It was Tandy who had the worst of it, as he had to borrow the whole of north-east Africa, the Sudan and the Congo before he found what he was looking for – an area marked 'jungle'.

'Six bloomin' cig issues it cost me,' he said.

'But why did you do it, Tandy?' I asked.

'I told you – I didn't like to think of him spending his life in that cage. Besides, it gave me something to live for.'

'To live for!' I exclaimed with some heat. 'With all the wonders of God's world around you, you speak of needing something to live for!'

He stared at his feet and for a moment, absurd as it may

seem, almost gave me the impression that he did not suppose I could understand what he meant.

'Well, carry on, Tandy,' I said, a little sharply, 'what did you get up to next?'

His next move was to obtain his ordinary uniform by telling the sergeant in charge of the store that he was 'sick of mucking round in "blues" like a blank, blank wounded hero and wanted to look normal-like and see a bit of life'. The war was dragging to its end; regulations were steadily slackening and no one cared whether Tandy wore blue or khaki. Now, in normal dress, practically recovered and free to come and go in the hospital much as he pleased, he knew he was in danger of being sent to the convalescent camp on the sea-coast. He had no time to waste.

He had made a point of offering his services to the matron and M.O. so they began to rely on him, were not over-eager for his discharge and were always sending him on errands down into the town. These did not usually take him further than the Italian or German hospitals in the Street of the Prophets, but he was sometimes sent to headquarters to deliver a letter or pick up papers. Once past the barrier, he would spend all the time he dared lingering near the Orderly Office. As soon as he saw the officer go out, Tandy would put his head round the door. If there was anyone else inside, he would mumble: 'Beg pardon, sir, just looking for the major, sir,' and close the door quickly, knowing no one would bother to follow him. If the office were empty, he would tip-toe rapidly to the desk and take a single Movement Order form, stamp it and slip away leaving everything apparently untouched. In this way he managed to get half a dozen forms, a copy of the Orderly Officer's signature and a lorry Work Book. He said that some instinct always told him how long he might safely stay in the room.

'When I do a snatch, guv,' he said, 'I feel a sort of excitement like I was a bit above everything and can see just how far I can go. I always feel safe when I do a snatch. It's only when I go outside my line that things go wrong.'

He did not know at what point he would get beyond British frontier control, so he pocketed the Movement Orders and decided to fill them up for each new stage of the journey as required. For this purpose he would need a typewriter. He also needed a lorry, tins of petrol to get him across the desert regions and some of those six-pound tins of bully beef in case he had difficulty in getting camel-meat for the tiger. He knew the risk of stealing everything from one source so he took from the hospital only one tin of petrol and an old Remington portable that had been standing unused in the matron's office for months and was not missed until a fortnight after Tandy's mysterious disappearance.

He had been trained as a chauffeur-mechanic at Borstal but made no use of his knowledge until, being called up, he was set to drive a lorry. He knew all about army lorries and instead of stealing just any lorry that might be parked in the town and would certainly be missed within the hour, he went one moonlit Friday night to a dump of derelict lorries in the Mustrara Quarter and repaired one of the covered trucks for himself. Moonlight in Jerusalem is more brilliant than most English winter daylight and Tandy was able to do the work with the aid merely of an electric torch. These lorries had had their tanks drained and were in such a condition that the only guard was one of the local volunteer soldiers. This individual did not wake up until Tandy had filled the tank from his purloined tin and was driving the truck out of the gate, and he probably thought it wiser not to report the theft. No one knew that a lorry was missing until Tandy himself confessed to taking one.

He drove it straight to the Polish Family Canteen where he 'effected an entry' to use his own words, and loaded up with a hundred six-pound cans of bully beef. Petrol was going to be a less easy matter. Petrol dumps were much more closely guarded than disused lorries and he decided to wait until he reached some of the remote desert dumps where surveillance was less strict.

I can remember the stir created by the theft from the Polish Canteen. For months it was laid at the door of the Irgun on the grounds that no British troops would steal bully beef if there was anything else to be stolen. It seemed odd to me that Tandy was concerned only with storing up food for the tiger.

'You didn't take anything for yourself?' I quizzed him. 'Not even a tin of salmon or a box of biscuits?'

'No, guv. What with the bully and the petrol there wouldn't't've been room. I had to give the tiger a bit'uv breathing space. 'Sides, I'm not adverse to bully m'self. I'm used to it. But I did take a case of char. Out in the desert you get a trifle dry so you keep stopping to brew up with the hot water from the tank.'

'And how did you make the Work Book tally with the lorry you stole?'

He wrote with his hand on the air: 'Bit of scribing,' he said and obviously the matter had been so easily dealt with he did not think it worth explaining further.

'Well, and what did you do next?'

He then told me how he took the lorry to the services all-night filling station and there as a bona-fide driver with papers all in order, he got petrol, water, and air.

'And then,' he said, 'I fetched the tiger.'

'That must have been a job.'

'Easy as kiss your hand. Shinned over the wall, forced keepers' hut, got keys, opened door, drove in lorry, put lump of bully in lorry, opened cage, stuck the bridge in, put the other end in the lorry and waited. Tiger walked across just to see. I pulled down bridge, slammed up the lorry back and Bob's your uncle. All done inside quarter 'ar.'

'It sounds easy enough as you tell it,' I said, 'but I think you showed remarkable ingenuity.'

He ducked his head modestly and said: 'Aw, it was nothing.'

I wanted to read him a lecture on the duty of every man to expend his talents for good, but for the life of me I could think of no use for Tandy's talents save that to which he applied them.

And so, there he was with a hundred tins of bully beef, a case of tea, a typewriter and a tiger in a lorry. While he was in the zoo he looked round for anything useful that he might take with the tiger and he took the water-trough from the cage and also a long-handled broom and pan that would enable him to clean the lorry from the front seat. He also found a hunk of camel-meat which he threw in to quiet the creature which was knocking itself suspiciously against the walls of its confined new quarters.

'Do you think the tiger was happy in that lorry?' I asked him.

'P'r'aps not,' Tandy agreed, 'but he was only there tem'pry. Besides, whenever I got a clear road, I opened a sort of trap-door at the back and gave him a blow through. That old tiger seemed to know.'

'Know what?'

'That I was taking him home.'

I had a revelation to make to Mr Tandy on that point, but I thought I would save it up until I got the whole story out of him.

'And now your troubles began?' I suggested. When he

[131]

seemed surprised I explained: 'That long journey right down through Egypt and the Sudan into the Congo!'

'Piece of cake,' he said. 'First thing I came on, outside Rajah, was a big petrol dump. I'd heard about it afore; I knew it was there. I just brought the truck up against the wire and used it to get over. Then I loaded fifty tins on top and tied them all neat and careful like we'd been taught. Then in Sinai I picked up a convoy and just tacked m'self on. I got over the frontier with the rest – didn't even have to show my Movement Order. Pity! I'd made a nice job of it. Then I made out a nice new order for Wadi Halfa and when I got to Assuit, I tacked on to another convoy that was taking supplies to Khartoum. Not a question asked all the way.'

'But what about the tiger?'

'Always fed him at night. He soon got used to the truck and there was nothing around him to worry him. He seemed to like the dark and he didn't pad about half so much. Tigers is queer creatures. Never a roar out of him; he'd make a sort of coughing noise sometimes but I always managed to cover that up. Said I'd got catarrh. I always parked my lorry well away from the rest, then I'd clean it out and feed and water the tiger. He'd got used to me in no time and didn't seem to mind me poking around a bit. 'Course I was always very careful. At times he looked so sleepy you'd think you could stroke him – but I didn't take no risks. Sometimes he'd have a fit of throwing himself about and chaps'ud say "What's all that din?" but no one ever thought it was a tiger in a truck. If they heard a cough at night they'd think it was a jackal – you get them in the desert. And I told everyone my truck was loaded up with skins to make rugs for the officers' mess at Khartoum.'

Tandy looked at me as though I ought to see the significance of that piece of cunning, but I was only puzzled. I laughed: 'You mean, if they happened to see the tiger, they'd just think it was an animated carpet?'

'Not that,' said Tandy seriously. 'But after a while the heat being a bit much in them parts, the truck began to pong. The smell was sort of tigerish.'

'I see. I must admit you thought of everything. I suppose this forethought was essential in your earlier profession?'

He hung his head and mumbled: 'Suppose so, Padre.'

His troubles started after he separated from the convoy at Khartoum. Until then he had had all the advantages of being led from one point to another with large desert camps and food, water and petrol issues, and companionship. After Khartoum he was on his own.

'But it was better for the tiger,' he said. 'No need to hide him now.'

He slipped away from the others when they camped on the outskirts of Khartoum. He decided that to be sure of water it would be safer to follow the White Nile rather than attempt any short cuts by branching off into the desert towards El Obeid. He took this journey in easy stages, stopping at the Nile-side villages for food and sleeping each night under the truck. So far the trip had cost him nothing; now he had to break into his savings to pay for beans, bread and fresh drinking water. Sometimes in the larger villages he was able to buy petrol but this was not often. Before he reached Juba he had used a dozen tins and the tiger had got through half the corned-beef. Meat, even camel-meat, is rare in that part of the Arab world and Tandy was able to get fresh food for the tiger only when some beast had died in a village. The heat down there must have been intense and the poor animal, shut up in its dark box, plagued by flies and mosquitoes, could not have been happy. Tandy began to worry about it. It was obviously suffering from lack of air, light and exercise. It had become lethargic and its coat was losing its gloss. He had found it impossible to keep the truck perfectly clean and it now needed a good scrub through. The situation was eased by the fact that there was no need to keep the tiger's presence a secret and when he came to a large, important-looking village on the Sudanese frontier, Tandy required the headman to be brought to him. When the headman and most of the village were gathered round him, he made a speech in the atrocious pigeon-Arabic which he had picked up in Palestine. He explained that he was on a very important mission to the Great White Chief of Uganda and was taking him a tiger as a gift from the King of England. The tiger was suffering from the heat and its cramped quarters and if the villagers would help improve its conditions they would be richly rewarded next time the representative of the Sudanese Government passed that way.

I cannot think how Tandy made himself understood. Arabic alters so much from country to country that in the southern Sudan it could bear no more than a resemblance to the language of Palestine but, whatever they made of him, the villagers were enthusiastic about Tandy, his tiger and the promised reward. They willingly set-to and under his supervision made a strong wooden cage. When they saw that Tandy was going to open the doors at the back of the truck they crowded round with excited curiosity, so he realized with some surprise that they had no idea what a tiger was. As soon as they saw the great beast lying there, blinking in the first sunlight it had seen for weeks, a great cry of wonder and admiration rose from the villagers. Strangely enough they showed no fear.

'You'd almost think they'd never seen a blinking tiger before,' said Tandy.

He got them to lift the cage to the truck level; then the

tiger was tempted by a piece of raw meat to enter in. Tandy quickly closed and latched the cage door and there the tiger lay purring and chewing at the meat while the natives crowded close to watch. Tandy cleaned out the truck. That job finished, the tiger was put back, cage and all, so Tandy was not only able to drive with the back of the truck open but to reach without danger the more distant tins of bully.

'Better for all concerned,' he said. He gave the headman a Sudanese pound and set off again.

'And what was the country like?' I asked, being one always interested in the beauties of nature.

'Smashing,' said Tandy, 'I could see I was going in the right direction – getting away from all that desert into the lushy sort of scenery that's just right for tigers. And the people, too – you could see them turning into real blacks just as they ought to be. I'd been getting a bit worried by the desert. There seemed so much of it, I began to think I'd never get to the jungle, but now I knew everything was in order.'

When he crossed into Uganda he began to come on white settlers who were farming and ranching on the extensive grasslands. They treated Tandy well, helped him to feed and water the tiger, and gave him the directions he needed; but his story that he was taking the tiger to the zoo at Elisabethville must have aroused suspicion. It was then that inquiries began to get through to the Cairo G.H.Q. about a British private in Central Africa with a tiger in a truck. These were not taken seriously and it was only a month later, when Tandy gave himself up, that anyone bothered to check up on his adventures.

The white settlers asked him so many questions that he began to get worried and after a while avoided the settlements. He was again surprised by the interest the tiger aroused (after all, he thought, weren't people in Uganda surrounded by tigers?) but was afraid to arouse suspicion by asking anyone questions he might reasonably be expected to be able to answer himself. Had he done so, he might have discovered much sooner what I later had to tell him: though what he would have done then, I do not know.

He had now got out of Uganda into the Congo and could see in the distance the dark verge of the forest that was his goal. He kept well away from any signs of civilized life. The country was rich and watered; he managed to get plenty of bananas and flour from the native villages, and the tiger was eating its way through the last ten cans of bully. The petrol was getting low but with the jungle in sight, Tandy was no longer worried and seemed not to care how he was going to make the return journey himself. At last, some time after first sighting it, he came to the verge of the forest, but he was not content to loose the tiger there. He thrust the truck into the mass of jungle vegetation for about a mile before he decided the moment had come to open the gate of the cage. He stopped the truck in a small clearing where the sunlight was able to penetrate through the leaves and went round to take a last look at his tiger. The creature was, he says, restless and sniffing at the air as though excited by smells it had never smelt before, and it started to claw at the wooden bars of the cage.

'Y'd just think it knew this was where it belonged,' said Tandy. 'I didn't want to keep him in there a moment longer, but I looked at him a minute and I said: "Well, here we are, Tiger, old chap – Home Sweet Home for you now. Goodbye," I said and I opens the cage and hops it back into the driving-seat. Then I hears him jump out and I looks round and there he is standing in the sunlight just like a picture. Never saw such a sight – pure black and gold he looked and just right there with all those big trees and the leaves like fans and

[136]

flowers bigger than the ones on seed-packets. "Good-bye, old chap," I shouts but he takes no notice of me. He gives a shake of his head and a swish of his tail and off he streaks into the leaves and is gone in a sec. And after that I didn't know what to do. I drove back to the first farm I saw and gave myself up. I didn't care what happened. I felt so lost without that there tiger, I didn't care much what they did with me. The chap at the farm cabled Khartoum and they sent instructions to put me on the road back – and back I goes like a lamb. I didn't care. I took the tiger home and that's all that matters.'

'You feel very pleased with yourself, don't you, Tandy?' I said. I didn't want to be uncharitable but his smug expression got my hackles up.

'Oh, I don't know,' he said, trying to look modest.

'You feel you've been quite a Good Samaritan, don't you, Tandy – robbing this poor little zoo, robbing the Polish Family Canteen, stealing a lorry, stealing petrol, imposing on people all the way down through Africa . . .'

'I did it for the tiger,' he wailed. 'Truth, I did, Padre! I couldn't see the poor brute stuck in that cage all its life.'

'And you think the tiger will be happy there in the African jungle!'

'Well, why shouldn't he be? – that's his home, ain't it?'

'No, it isn't, Tandy,' I said severely, feeling he must be taught a lesson, 'there are no tigers in Africa. The tiger is a native of India – not of Africa.'

'You mean it'ud be alone there? It wouldn't find another tiger?'

'No, it wouldn't find another tiger – and I'm not sure it could survive there. Not sure at all. You took the poor creature on that terrible journey and turned it adrift in a

[137]

strange place where it might suffer a lingering death from starvation, or fall a prey to . . .'

I had to pause because Tandy was staring at me with his mouth open and two heavy tears welling out of his eyes.

'Now! No nonsense, Tandy,' I said irritably, but he started sobbing. He put his head down on his hands and wept so noisily, you might have thought, if you did not know him, that his heart was going to break.

London, 1946.

Twilight of the Gods

Twilight of the Gods

Elizabeth Jackson was taking a holiday alone for the first time for eight years. Something in her appearance – an air of well-meaning, perhaps – had got her quickly through the Customs and off the airport. Now she was being driven towards the boarding-house in which she had found a room. The journey had been much easier than friends had led her to anticipate. She did not imagine that some virtue in herself made it easier, but she did think she was rather a lucky woman. A woman who had not only got safely from London to Dublin, but was fortunate in her marriage, in her children and in her present freedom from worry about the children. They were in good hands. No need to fear unduly a sudden blow by telegram or newspaper headline – so there was hope of shaking off in time this preoccupation with the problems of housewifery in England. To make a start she gazed out from the taxi at the foods in the shops – at hams, tongues, bacon, sausages, baskets of eggs and bottles of whiskey, and reflected that she could, if she wished, go in and buy any of them. As a result she realized she did not want to buy them and there was a slight relaxing of tension in her solar plexus.

The taxi, leaving the shops behind, passed Georgian houses that stood in unbroken rows, mellowed by time but flawless and bland as cream-fed cats.

Elizabeth, smiling, supposed the cream idea came from the new paint – these milky porticos, front doors and window-frames decorating the acres of rose-pink brick; these occasional doors the colour of a greengage or a red grape or a foggy blue horizon – and over all of them the bloom of the sweet, nostalgic evening in autumn.

'New net curtains,' she whispered. Then added: 'Enjoy it.' Something that had been rattling in her head for months began to settle down. The sense of urgency that in post-war England made her get out the latch-key a hundred yards before reaching her house, began to fade and she admitted for the first time for years the possibility of leisure to enjoy.

She watched the houses, comforted by them, until something went wrong with their proportions. The porticos became too weighty, the steps over-important – then, of a sudden, classicism had had its day and the taxi stopped in a terracotta square wrought, during the Gothic revival, with the fogs and fancies of the Middle Ages. The light, too, had changed. The earlier peach-bloom had deepened to a damson bloom and hung over the trees like smoke from a damp fire.

When she lifted out her heavy suitcase, the taxi-driver said: 'I'll carry it up for you.'

She looked at him in astonishment, almost embarrassment, as though he were an innocent among taxi-drivers of whom she might be taking advantage, but he smiled as though the kindness were a personal matter being done for the sheer pleasure of helping her.

'There y'are now,' he said as he put down the bag at the top of the steps. 'And I hope y'll enjoy y'visit.'

The maids in the boarding-house had this same unfamiliar willingness to help, to please. Elizabeth, unpacking in a small back room, felt herself grow inwardly tender like an invalid who, after struggling alone against an indifferent world, collapses when kindness comes. 'In England,' she thought, 'we're all becoming invalids. We're all suffering from obsessional neurosis. We're all persecuted because we've come down in the world.'

The chambermaid thumped on the door and said: 'Dinner at seven o'clock.'

Down in the dim basement dining-room, she was put at a table with another Englishwoman. She was so astonished by the meat put on her plate – so much of it and with a richness she had forgotten – she glanced smiling round the room; but everyone else was taking it for granted, so she held her tongue.

Right at the end of the meal, the Englishwoman asked her if she were staying long.

'Only a week,' she said, glad to talk. 'Then I go for a week to friends at Boyle.'

'Really! Only a week!' the woman rolled her napkin and pushed it into a ring marked "Mrs Potts". 'Most of us are residents.'

'I know I was lucky to get here. The hotels were full, but . . .' Elizabeth smiled a propitiatory smile, 'I was highly recommended.'

'I'm sure you were,' Mrs Potts's eyes flickered over Elizabeth's hands that were redder than a lady's hands should be in Ireland, 'I'm sure you were.'

'There are a lot of English people here.'

'Indeed, yes. All the nicer people are coming to live in Ireland.'

'So I gather!' Elizabeth spoke not without sharpness. 'The Irish call it "The Retreat from Moscow".'

Mrs Potts nodded complacently: 'They're quite right,' she said and left the table.

The diners went one after the other upstairs to their rooms. Elizabeth, shut again into her sliver of a room, moved round restlessly. She was familiar with this determined privacy, this gas-fire with its slot-meter, the wash-hand basin behind a screen, the single divan where, with hot-water bottle and book, one escaped from chilly solitude into the circle of the reading-lamp. She had known all of them before her marriage and now, for the first time for years, she glanced after her girlhood and saw how far it had receded. She did not want to be alone.

Since her marriage the world had changed from pre- to post-war. She, she supposed, had changed with it. She was still young enough to see her early youth as something taken from her by circumstances rather than by age. Before the war, she reflected, one anticipated the future with excitement, now one kept one's mind off it. That fact had somehow changed everything and she blamed it for a sort of deathly inertia that descended on her too often these days. Before it could descend again she took out her notebook. Within was a list of names and addresses of people in Dublin – friends of friends, all strangers, better left until tomorrow. Beneath them was the one familiar name of Flora Beer.

When someone had suggested she should look up Flora, she had murmured with enthusiasm and added the address to her list – but something within her had winced.

Yet Flora had never actually hurt her.

They had attended the same academy of music. Flora had been the only child of a famous pianist who died young. Every newcomer to the academy had started at her name and asked could she be . . . ? Yes, she was. She was somebody without effort; the sole inheritor of her father's talent, money and circle of admirers. Elizabeth saw her as living in the sort of world then being exploited by romantic novelists – a world where everyone had genius, beauty and emotional disturbances on an Olympian scale.

She and Elizabeth were the only two women studying the pianoforte at the time, so, sitting together in theory class, Flora extended towards Elizabeth a patronizing friendliness. Elizabeth, made to be a 'constant nymph', was glad to sit in the dressing-room of Flora's life and hear her talk about parties and affairs.

'What have I to complain about?' Elizabeth asked herself now. 'That she could have altered my life, and didn't bother? Well, my life came all right of itself. I've nothing to grumble about.'

Flora had long hair and on the night when she washed it, she would ring and tell Elizabeth to come round and make tea. Sometimes Elizabeth, knowing where Flora was going, would stand at a safe distance to gaze at the dazzle of an open doorway, or a lighted first-floor window behind which figures moved. She never got any closer than that. Once she had, in sheer desperation of loneliness, dared to ring Flora's flat and heard Flora answer crossly: 'Sorry, can't talk to you now. Got someone here,' and put down the receiver so that Elizabeth felt like a remote star, a black cinder of a star poised friendless in the desolation of space.

'Well, what did I expect?' Nothing, nothing; no, it wasn't that. It was – ah, now she was getting nearer it – it was that Flora, with all her advantages, was a complaining girl. That enviable world was always going sour on her. She did not repay worship. Still, that was not, if one were to be honest, an explanation of a persistent resentment. 'I suppose I'm jealous,' said Elizabeth, 'I suppose, in spite of everything, I'm still jealous. I still feel a failure because I didn't get inside. I ought to be ashamed of myself.'

The chambermaid came in to turn down the bed. 'Shall I light the fire for you?' she said.

'No, I'm going out. I'm going for a walk.' As she put on her coat she suddenly spoke Flora's address aloud then, to excuse herself, asked the girl where it was. It was not more than five hundred yards away.

The streets were dimly lit – the first sign of shortage yet. The lights in the hallways of Georgian houses revealed fanlights that were indeed fans of glass spread open above the opulent porticoes. Beside them were the lighted windows, the haze of net curtaining beyond which figures moved. Flora might be in any of these rooms. She had never been one to stay at home.

Elizabeth was still uncertain whether she intended visiting Flora, but when she came to the street she turned into it. It was impressive enough, but the front door of the house was shabby and covered with names. It stood ajar. Within was a bare hallway filled by a child's perambulator, half a dozen bicycles and a strong smell of cooking. At the top of the stairs, five flights up, Elizabeth came upon the inscription: 'Miss Flora Beer, Concert Pianist'. Somewhere beyond it a Chopin Valse was being played with fury. It stopped the instant she touched the bell push.

Elizabeth, having in mind a picture of Flora as she had known her – the delicate pink-and-white face, the dark hair dressed like a ballet dancer's – stared bewildered at the haggard blonde woman who threw open the door. The woman stared back and said in exasperated tones: 'Do you want anything?'

'But you *are* Flora! I'm Elizabeth – I used to be Elizabeth Finchen.'

'Oh, yes,' said Flora with no pleasure and no surprise, 'do come in.'

'Perhaps, if you're busy, I'd better not. I thought you might be washing your hair.'

'Washing my hair! I don't wash my own hair.' Flora's laugh broke a little the surface of her anger – if it were anger – and her voice grew milder: 'Come in,' she repeated with no more than impatience. 'You don't expect me to talk on the door-step.'

They went down a narrow passage with plywood walls into a room that had two solid walls and two of plywood. It just took the upright piano, the card-table set for a meal for two, a basket-chair, a standard lamp with a fringe and a couch heaped with cushions.

'Don't look at this place,' said Flora, 'I rent it furnished.'

On the mantelpiece were stacks of dusty letters and post-cards, an open telegram standing on its edge and two gilt-lettered invitations that were, Elizabeth noticed when she got near enough, over a year old.

'Sit down,' said Flora and herself knelt to put pennies in a meter.

'Don't light the fire for me. I'm not a bit cold.'

'Of course I'll light it. I'd have lit it before but I forgot, playing.'

Elizabeth, in the basket-chair, felt less of an intruder as the warmth touched her ankles. She raised her glance and looked at Flora, settled now on the divan under the lamp, who looked back with critical eyes and said: 'You haven't changed much. Tell me what you're doing here?'

'I was ordered to take a holiday—'

'Really!' Flora's laugh had a sharper edge than Elizabeth remembered. 'How nice for you! Are you ill or something?'

'No, not really ill. Just a bit shagged. We all are.'

'And I suppose that's why you're all taking holidays? This place is crowded with English – a proper invasion!'

[147]

'I'm only staying a fortnight.'

'Oh, everyone's only staying a fortnight – but we're pretty sick of them. They eat like pigs and put the prices up.'

'The Irish don't seem to mind us, and it's their country. What about you? Don't you count as a visitor?'

Flora looked at Elizabeth and now observed her. It seemed to come into her head, as it came into Elizabeth's, that they were on the verge of a quarrel. She swallowed in her throat and a bright, effortful sociability diluted her earlier manner. She did not reply to Elizabeth's question but said: 'I haven't seen you since I left the academy – how long ago? Ten years? Lord, yes, ten years. Did you say you were married?'

'I got married in 1938,' Elizabeth was breathless with response. 'I married John Jackson. He's a teacher. I met him in the holidays at home in Manchester, and now we have three children. It wasn't easy for me to get away. It seemed impossible at first but, in the end, John's mother took the twins and a friend took Betty, and we decided to shut up the house . . .'

Flora's eyelids drooped over her eyes and Elizabeth, conscious of boring her, trailed off lamely: 'John's gone to a boarding-house. Not much fun for him.'

Flora's eyelids continued to droop. The light on her jaw-line touched a crust of make-up. At last she sighed deeply: 'That's what I need – a holiday. But – oh, I don't know. It's all so difficult.'

Elizabeth, aware of the card-table set for two, took this opportunity to ask: 'What keeps you here?'

'I don't know,' Flora glanced round vaguely as though there might be an explanation at her elbow. 'Everything's so difficult – such an effort.'

'Have you any friends here?'

'Friends? Well, a few. There are plenty of English people

living here now. All my friends are English. The Irish are all right but, really, they're so provincial. Yes, there's quite a little group of us. Like refugees. Like White Russians.' Her voice lifted as she asked: 'Do you think I've changed much? You didn't recognize me?'

'Not at first—'

'It's my hair. I had to do something about it. You know, I was so ill! I couldn't stand the strain of the war and my hair started to go grey – just strain, you know! Nerves and strain. I had to do something about it. After all, I'm only thirty-four.'

'Are you? But I'm thirty-six.'

Flora laughed: 'And I used to think I was the elder.'

Elizabeth opened her lips, paused, then said: 'How long have you lived here?'

'Since 1940. I evacuated myself just in time. I suppose you had to do war work?'

'Not much. I had the twins, and then I started Peter—'

'Oh, yes, people with children got out of everything, didn't they? Nice for them.'

'My husband was in the army. He was sent to the Western Desert.'

Flora was staring at her nails with a petulant look; some moments passed before she glanced up and murmured: 'Really! The desert? How tiresome! But you're a tough little thing. I remember you used to live in London on about twopence a week. I felt so sorry for you. I used to befriend you, didn't I?' she laughed, 'I gave you cups of tea. I'm afraid my little income doesn't go so far these days.'

'But it must be pleasant living here?'

'It's hell. This place is a backwater. People here are so critical of anyone who's a bit advanced – and I'm very sensitive. I always was very sensitive. You know how people upset me! – and here they're so self-satisfied! and everyone's such a little somebody! They're such a crowd of wits, my dear! Really, I can't tell you. They make me sick.'

'But you're still a pianist. Me – I've scarcely opened a piano for six years. And here you are giving concerts!'

'Concerts! Well, not many. I'm not really strong enough to do much of that,' she broke off, listened and asked abruptly: 'Did you hear anything?'

'No, but if you're expecting someone, I'd better go.'

'Don't go.'

Elizabeth almost cried out: 'But I want to go.' She sat restlessly for a moment, then said: 'I think I must go . . .'

'No, don't go – please,' Flora's tone and manner changed suddenly to pleading and Elizabeth, knowing herself lost, relaxed into her chair. She knew Flora's gift of pathos.

'But who are you waiting for?' she had to ask.

'A friend. You may know him – Ralph Peacock?'

'You know I never knew anyone.'

'No, but you may have heard the girls talking about him at the academy. He was an actor . . . enormously good-looking.'

'Is he acting over here?'

'He can't get anything here. They don't appreciate him. This place is the end.'

'What's he doing here, then?'

'Well . . .' Flora's voice trailed away and she stared at her fingernails: 'Some situations are beyond our control, aren't they?' She smiled mysteriously at her purple nail-polish and when Elizabeth asked no further questions, began picking at one nail so the polish came off like a shell. She giggled: 'How filthy one's nails are underneath when you take the polish off. Haven't you noticed?'

'I don't use it.'

'Can't you get it? England must be hell.'

'You know, I'd much rather go. I'm sure Ralph Peacock wouldn't want to find a visitor here.'

'He probably wouldn't – but it will be very good for him. We were going to a flick; and now look at the time! He thinks I've been sitting here whimpering since seven o'clock. He'll find he's wrong.'

'But surely he won't come here now?'

After a pause Flora said: 'He lives here. He's got nowhere else to go.'

While she occupied herself with picking off her nail-polish, Elizabeth reflected that for Flora life behind the lighted windows still went on. She might be blanched and raddled, have curls like brass and live in a shabby, plywood flat, yet she kept her right to the romantic world into which Elizabeth had never even set a foot. The silence was dragging out into minutes when Flora suddenly stiffened; a moment later Elizabeth heard a key turn in the front-door lock. A heavy, blundering step came down the passage. The sitting-room door fell open and a man entered:

'Hello!' he said, 'a visitor! This is a pleasant change.'

Flora did not look up or speak. Elizabeth introduced herself: 'I'm an old friend of Flora's—'

'An old friend of Flora's! Well, well! I didn't know Flora had any friends, much less "old ones".' He turned to the card-table: 'What about some food?'

Flora, intent on fingernails, still said nothing.

'Sulks, as usual!' Ralph said and tried to sit on the couch beside her. She would not move. 'Shove along, sister,' he said and, pushing her easily up into the corner, took two-thirds of the seat for his wide buttocks and straddled legs. It was clear he had been handsome at one time, but now he looked like some object soaked in liquid until it had become pulpy. His large, dark eyes moved in his head like the dull, bloodshot eyes of an ox. They turned restlessly round the room then fixed themselves on Elizabeth: 'You're English,' he said.

Flora now spoke, coldly, as from a great distance: 'Don't worry. She's nobody. She can't do you any harm.'

He grunted and moved his eyes round to Flora at his side as though he found it difficult to turn his neck: 'What about some food?' he repeated.

'Couldn't you find anyone to feed you? You've exhausted the lot of them, now, haven't you? They're all sick to death of you, aren't they? You've gone round throwing your weight about and getting drunk and breaking up people's parties, until there isn't one person left who'll have you in his house. But you still expect to turn up here at ten o'clock and find a meal waiting for you. Well, you won't get it.'

'There! There!' he patted her amiably on the back. 'Get Ralphie his supper for the last time.'

She sat as before, then, of a sudden, her head jerked up and she gave him a startled look: 'What do you mean – the last time?'

'Well, perhaps not the last, but very nearly the last time.'

She stared at him and said breathlessly: 'I don't know what you're talking about.'

He lay back on the couch and laughed to himself.

'I suppose you're drunk?' she said.

'Not more than usual. I'm just trying to break it to you gently, dearie, that my uncle's dead. There was a wire waiting for me at the post office this afternoon.'

'You've got the fifty thousand?' she asked, her voice dying in her throat.

'Not yet, but it's coming. The lawyer's sending me something on account. Isn't that nice! And you won't be bothered with Ralphie any more.'

'But you're not leaving me?'

'What do you think? I haven't put up with you just for the fun of it.'

'After all I've done for you!'

'After all I've done for you!' he mimicked her tones so they were ludicrous with self-pity.

She flushed and, lifting her whole arm, struck him across the face. Ralph's expression did not change but he sat slowly upright. Flora tried to leap out of her seat but she was too tightly wedged. As she leant forward, Ralph caught her arm and twisted it up behind her back.

'Say you're sorry,' he said gently. When she did not answer he jerked her arm upward so her breath escaped in a thin wail. 'Say you're sorry,' he repeated gently as before.

Elizabeth, unnerved by a glimpse of Flora's red, strangled face, between strands of yellow hair, got to her feet. 'You really are hurting her,' she said, but the others took no notice. Realizing she was nothing but a spectator in the room, she backed against the mantelpiece and stood uncertainly until, not knowing what else to do, she sat down again.

Flora's resistance broke at last and she screamed: 'Stop it. If you injure my arm, I can't play.'

'Just say you're sorry.'

'I'm sorry, curse you!' When Ralph released her, Flora leant back panting in her corner and spoke against her own lack of breath: 'I've kept you for two years . . . when no one else would have you . . . Now you think your money will make all the difference. . . .'

'And won't it? It has already. Who do you think had just been celebrating with me? And at the Shelbourne Rooms for all to see?'

'Who?' she asked hoarsely.

'Inez.'

Flora's ruined face seemed to collapse with fury. Even Ralph moved on guard. Elizabeth, afraid of the single-minded selfishness of these two people, knew she herself had not only not the right, but not even the means to exist in this air. Their ruthlessness seemed to her like a separate organ that gave them a power she lacked. She would have escaped – simply walked out of the door – if she had had the courage to risk attracting their attention. She sat on, watching them like someone who can only wait for a storm to subside. She and Ralph both looked at Flora. Flora did and said nothing. Her face slowly remoulded itself and when at last she spoke, her manner was off-hand.

'People like Inez don't cost much,' she said. 'You could buy a number of them for fifty thousand.'

'I could buy almost anything,' Ralph smiled as he relaxed. 'Except perhaps – a passage to England?'

'Who wants it?' Ralph's manner changed suddenly to the defensive. 'I don't see you hurrying back.'

'No, because there's nothing to stop me. It's different when you're trapped here.'

'People live very well here with a bit of cash. Look at the chaps who're living like lords on two thousand a year! They're the new aristocracy. Nice house, servants, hunting, shooting, fishing, plenty to eat – it'd suit me down to the ground. And think of all the girls I'd meet! Virgin soil, you might say. Young girls! Lovely girls! Girls who know nothing about me. Ummm!' He drew in his breath like someone sucking an orange.

Flora gave him a look of disgust. 'In this place,' she said, 'everyone knows everything about everyone – and there are a lot of English people who aren't too keen to know a deserter.'

Ralph turned in his seat and looked at Flora as though there must be something peculiarly ridiculous about her: 'You were pretty keen,' he said.

'I felt sorry for you.'

'Did you now! And I felt sorry for you. Just two lonely people, weren't we, dearie? Everyone was sick to death of you and sick to death of me – so we felt sorry for each other and just naturally gravitated. But *I'm* being given a fresh start. Isn't that nice! – and aren't you glad? It calls for a celebration.' Ralph rose and started hunting round the room. 'Where've you hidden it?'

'There isn't any.'

Ralph went out of the room. There were sounds of his hunting about in other parts of the flat.

Elizabeth took the opportunity to say: 'Now I really must go.' Flora did not glance up or reply. Elizabeth was moving quietly towards the door when Ralph returned with a gin bottle and three glasses: 'Hey!' he pushed at her chest with the bottle. 'Go back to your seat. We're celebrating.'

Elizabeth was about to say she must go when she felt her repetition of the necessity was becoming ridiculous. As she paused, Ralph put down the glasses and splashed them full of gin.

'I can't drink that,' she said.

He put a glass into her hand: 'Take it, and don't argue.'

'Her husband fought in the Western Desert,' said Flora. 'Perhaps she'd rather not drink with a deserter.'

'Is that the trouble?' Ralph gave Elizabeth a push again so that she fell back into her chair. When he stood over her, his eyes upon her, she wondered if he were quite sane, but as he stared something died out in his glance. It was as though some central post had been pulled away from his confidence and his whole body began to sag like a tent. He swallowed his gin quickly and refilled his glass from the bottle in his hand: 'Is that the trouble? You don't want to drink with a bloody deserter?'

He was standing so closely over Elizabeth that she could smell the ancient stench of alcohol that came from his clothes. She said miserably at last: 'If you deserted – I suppose you had a good reason for it.'

'I had.' His speech was becoming clogged and, at the same time, dictatorial, 'I had. It wasn't my war.'

'I don't suppose it was anyone's war.'

'Oh, yes, it was. A lot of people wanted that war for their own ends.'

Elizabeth moved back her chair as best she could and looked up at Ralph's red, heavy face overhanging her: 'If you felt like that,' she said, 'you could have been a conscientious objector.'

Flora, sipping her gin in the background, said pleasantly: 'He was safer in the army. Too many of his friends were shut up under 18B.'

Ralph swung round bodily and stared at her: 'What if they were?' he mumbled. He moved uncertainly and somehow got himself back to the couch. When he was seated, he placed the bottle on the table as though afraid it would roll away, then he leant forward and gazed earnestly at Elizabeth. 'You know who started this war?' he asked. 'A lot of money-grubbing little Ikes with big noses. *You* know who I mean.'

'You're making a fool of yourself,' said Flora.

Ralph took no notice of her. 'I wasn't fighting any war for them,' he said. 'I wasn't fighting for them. Think of me! Just beginning to make a name for myself – just twenty-seven years of age – looks, talent, personality, money coming to me, all the women I wanted! Was I going to go and get killed for those little Ikes? Not likely! Out of this, Ralphie, I said. See?

[156]

And the first leave I got, I came over her and didn't go back again.'

'Couldn't they extradite you?' asked Elizabeth, bewildered.

'They tried. But I had friends. There were two sides in this war, you know – and over here quite a lot of important people weren't on yours. Does that surprise you? I expect it does. The English are always right, aren't they? Well, there were people here who thought otherwise and . . .' he raised his voice, 'they protected me.'

'Till they found you out,' murmured Flora.

Ralph drank deeply and refilled his glass. He repeated to himself: 'They protected me.'

'You were lucky,' said Elizabeth.

'What!' Ralph gazed at her sombrely. 'You think I'm lucky!' He touched his chest with thick, splayed fingers. 'I've been in this damned country for seven years. I'm sick of every stone in this town; I hate every bloody, self-righteous face in it. And what's happening to my career? I ask you – what's happening to it? There isn't a theatre in this place I'd be seen dead in!'

Flora laughed to herself.

Ralph stared into his glass. His voice broke as he said: 'I'll soon be too old to play heroes.'

Flora's laugh rose wildly: 'Oh dear!' she said, tears in her eyes, 'Oh dear! Oh dear!' She stretched herself with pleasure and smiled at Elizabeth. She said: 'I'm seriously thinking of coming back to England. I know it's tiresome, but it can't be as bad as this place. London is always exhilarating. And when I think of the parties, the theatres, the concerts, the intellectual life! Here, if you have fifty thousand, you can buy food! Just think of it! Food! You can buy food anywhere if you have the money. But in London – the fun!'

Elizabeth interrupted her quietly: 'I don't think you could come back.'

'Why not?'

'England has changed. You wouldn't know what it was all about.'

Ralph gave a guffaw of laughter; Flora turned pink: 'My dear child. You have never led any life worth talking about. You just don't know how to ride high above all the little people with their politics and restriction. I've always got what I wanted.'

Elizabeth smiled for the first time since she had entered the room.

Flora's voice rose tinny with annoyance: 'There's always a good time for those who're determined to get it—'

'And have the money to pay for it,' broke in Ralph. 'You won't get far with that face of yours and what's left of five pounds a week unearned income.'

'You talk about faces! You! You swollen pig! Too old to play heroes – I'll say you are! There isn't a theatrical agent in London who wouldn't burst out laughing at the sight of you.'

'I can afford to look how I like with fifty thousand—'

'Not on the stage. And when you pay back what you owe me—'

Ralph rose unsteadily from the couch: 'Pay back what I owe you!' he said quietly. 'Like hell I will!'

'You see if you don't.'

Elizabeth stood up, determined, and put her glass on the mantelpiece: 'I'm going.'

Ralph turned on her: 'That's right. Clear out – but take this money-grubbing bitch with you.' He caught Flora's arm and threw her off the couch into the middle of the room. 'Get out, both of you.'

'You just try and turn me out of my own flat!' Flora yelled.

Elizabeth edged round Ralph and slipped out of the door.

'You, too,' he bawled at Flora. 'Come on! Out you get!'

'You fool, you're mad drunk—'

'Mad drunk! Like hell! I want to be alone. I have to suffer alone and I'll be alone . . . Now, get out!'

As the front door closed after her, Elizabeth heard the thud of something falling and Flora shouting: 'I won't get out. I'll call the police . . .'

She ran down the stairs. None of the other doors opened. No heads looked out. Except for the uproar above there was silence.

Out in the empty, echoing streets, she could still hear the two voices, reduced at this distance to puppets' size. She gave one last glance up at the shadows moving behind the lighted attic window, then went back to her room, thankful to have a refuge.

London, 1947.

The Pantomime

The Pantomime

Mrs Jackson came almost as far as the dockyard gates with Anne, then she said: 'Now, go and tell the policeman who you are. He'll ring up your father and your father will come down.'

Anne had hoped her mother would come to the gates and ask the policeman herself. Her parents were on speaking terms just then. She and Marie had overheard a scene of reconciliation, with their father promising never to see Mrs Borrow again. That was all over, he said. Everything was going to be different in future. The children did not know whether to believe this because he had promised the same thing once before. Still, Anne said: 'Why won't you wait till he comes down?'

No. Mrs Jackson seemed shy. She wanted to hurry back to Marie who, from excitement at the thought of the pantomime, had developed a bilious attack before they set out. Anne went on alone to the high stone archway with its gilded coat-of-arms. An icy wind seemed to be blowing into and out of the dockyard at the same time. Everything under the hard, grey sky had been swept clean-edged by the wind. Anne stood holding on to her navy-blue school-hat while she waited for her father. The policeman was searching the kit of three sailors who were coming ashore, and when he had telephoned the designers' offices, he took no more notice of her.

Inside the dockyard, because of the broad, wide, cobbled spaces, everything seemed lighter and cleaner than outside. The low buildings stood far apart. In the distance were the masts and funnels of ships. Straight ahead, in dry dock, stood the old flagship – brilliantly fresh, brilliantly romantic with its colours and gold paint, its rows of little windows in the stern and all the intricacies of its rigging.

While she waited, Anne listened to the sailors making jokes with the policeman. The policeman was feeling inside a long, canvas bag: 'What have you got here?' he asked.

'Dirty washing, chum,' said the sailor in mild, humorous tones.

'Feels more like a tin of baccy to me,' said the policeman.

'You must have got hold of the buttons, chum,' said the sailor.

Anne watched anxiously, but the policeman was smiling: 'O.K. Pass along,' he said.

Her father appeared round the corner of a building. He was still adjusting the collar of his greatcoat as he came towards her. She knew he had worked in his office through the luncheon hour, eating only a sandwich, so he would be free to take his daughters to the pantomime. Mrs Jackson had said: 'That's the first time your father has put himself out to take you children anywhere.'

He asked: 'Where's Marie?'

'She was so excited she got a bilious attack.'

'What a pity! Well, no time to lose. Come along.' Outside the gate, he took Anne's hand: 'How cold you are!' he said, and rubbed her fingers briskly between his palms.

When she smiled up at him, she found him looking down at her with affectionate kindliness that reminded her of the time before the trouble started at home. The constraint that had grown between them suddenly broke down. Before they had reached the end of the long, high, bare dockyard wall, they were talking and laughing together with a freedom Anne seldom knew with her mother. If all the trouble really was over, she thought, it was going to be lovely.

People were crowding into the theatre for the matinée. Anne saw some girls from her school who stared to see her with her father. She clung on to his hand as he went to ask the man in the ticket-office to try and resell Marie's ticket. The man took it back at once: 'Full house today,' he said. Near by stood a group of children from a wealthy part of the town, all talking with unselfconscious exactness and confidence of pantomimes they had seen in past years. This was the first time Anne had been to the theatre. She turned away from the children, pretending they had made no impression on her.

'Come along,' said her father.

They went up a red-carpeted, cream-enamelled stairway marked 'Dress Circle'. At the top was a crescent-shaped passage from which doors opened on to the auditorium. Here some grown-ups were sitting on little gilt chairs while a string of small children were chasing one another excitedly through the shifting crowd. About half the dress-circle audience was already seated. Mr Jackson had cleverly bought seats early so they were in the front row. As he tilted down Anne's seat for her, the orchestra filed into position from a hole under the stage. Each man came doubled up but with his face lifted to look at the audience. Anne, her heart bursting with pride at being there in the front row with her father, gazed behind her at the rows of seats rising from three galleries of diminishing opulence, up and up to the great painted ceiling where cherubs played with trumpets, masks and wreaths. Anne, lifting her face right round, saw in the centre of the ceiling a crystal chandelier that dazzled the sight. In the cream-enamelled walls, flanked by gigantic plaster ladies who hid parts of themselves with pieces of drapery, the boxes were set like red-plush pockets. The largest was surmounted by a golden crown.

'Why is there a crown?' whispered Anne.

'Because it's the royal box.'

'You mean the queen sits in it?'

'Well, she would if she were here.'

'Is she ever here?'

Mr Jackson did not answer. He was gazing over the side at the seats in the stalls. Before the stage hung a safety-curtain painted with the shabby panorama of a garden. As soon as the orchestra had finished tuning up, it broke into a loud overture and the safety-curtain slid up. Behind were heavy crimson curtains tasselled with gold.

'Oh, Daddy, it's gorgeous!' said Anne, but Mr Jackson was not listening. He was gazing down intently at the people hurrying to their seats in the stalls. Anne, following his gaze, saw three ladies and two gentlemen walking round the front of the stalls and up the centre aisle. One of the ladies glanced up at him. He sat back in his seat with a sigh and opened the programme. The lights were dimming.

'Dear me!' he said, 'We've forgotten to look . . .' He held the programme sideways and read: ' "The Kitchen of the Red Lion Inn, London Town". This should be good.'

The overture stopped with a bang. A little jig began and faded as the curtain swung up and there were Dick and his cat at the kitchen sink singing 'Lots and lots and *lots* of dirty dishes'. It was a wonderful scene. Although a kitchen, it was enormous and painted red and had that fairy-tale quality you never see in real kitchens. The cat was very funny. He kept winking his enormous eyes and waltzing with his tail, and when Dick reminded him of the dishes, he showed that the easiest way to deal with them was to break them and throw them out of the window. The pile of broken crockery outside could be seen getting bigger and bigger.

The children in the audience became helpless with laughter. Anne, her eyelashes wet, turned to share her joy with her father, but he was not watching the fun: he was looking down at the stalls. Feeling her eyes on him, he turned his head, then nodded in front of him: 'Look, look, you're missing things. Here's the innkeeper's wife. Isn't she a scream? She's a man, really, and the little chap in the check plus-fours is the innkeeper. Aren't you enjoying it?'

'Oh, yes,' Anne whispered, and she watched the closing duet between Gloria, the innkeeper's lovely daughter, and Dick, who had decided to go abroad to seek his fortune. The next scene was on Highgate Hill, with Dick saying farewell to the city he loved. It would have been very sad indeed but for the excessive grief of the cat that turned it all into a joke; then, at the end, Dick heard the bells telling him he would become Lord Mayor of London. Anne forgot everything in envy of the bell-fairies who were, she saw, not fairies at all but real children no older than herself.

'Yes,' agreed Mr Jackson when she mentioned this, 'it says they're Madame Hilton's Dancing Pupils.' He moved restlessly for a moment or two, then said: 'I just want to go and speak to some friends. You stay here and read the programme like a good girl.'

He hurried off. Anne was left alone. The interval was a long one. She read the programme right through. Children pushed past her to buy lemonade and chocolate. Girls in black, with little white aprons, brought trays of tea and slices of seed cake. People who knew one another talked across her.

When she had finished the programme, she glanced round shyly. No one else seemed to have been left alone. Her cheeks burned and, to hide them, she leant over the balustrade and watched the activity in the stalls. She saw her father with the three ladies and two gentlemen she had watched come in. He was bending down talking to them, but he seemed disturbed and awkward and the others were not giving him much attention. One of the ladies stood up, and he and she went out through the nearest door. For the first time in her life, Anne recognized between two people a warmth of complete understanding. That, she knew, must be Mrs Borrow. Her father had broken his promise already! She felt, in a strange way, as though it were her own, his helplessness and the futility of his promises. She sat back in her seat and hid her face in the programme. She was worried by guilt and jealousy and the fact that she had understood what she had seen. She was worried especially by her understanding because she felt it a disloyalty to her mother.

It occurred to Anne that her mother would expect her to take some action, though she had no idea what it should be. She left her seat and went, nervously and cautiously, out into the brilliant foyer where people stood, crowded together, smoking, talking and laughing as though the whole audience were one big, jolly party to which she did not belong. She could see nothing of her father. She made her way down-stairs. At the bottom, a notice said 'Bar' and the bar door stood open. Inside, in a corner away from the other people, her father stood with Mrs Borrow. They were drinking something she thought must be wine.

She stopped, disconcerted, the more so because her mother disapproved of drink. On the few occasions, at Christmas or a birthday, that Mrs Jackson accepted a glass of sherry, she would sip it once or twice, then say: 'That sherry has taken my head,' as though sherry were a ravisher and better avoided. Now, as Anne stood at the bend of the stair, ready to disappear should her father glance her way, she thought that Mrs Borrow looked as though the wine had taken her head. She was leaning very close to Mr Jackson and the two were talking in whispers. It seemed to Anne that the red liquid in their glasses marked their relationship as something exceptional, and she knew she could do nothing about it.

She went back to her seat. When the lights dimmed again, her father had not returned; she sat through the next act alone. Because she kept looking round for him, she found it difficult to follow what was taking place on the stage. The scene was the garden of the Red Lion Inn where the king and aldermen had met to elect a new Lord Mayor. There were a lot of political jokes that made the grown-ups laugh and it all ended with a brilliant piece of trickery on the part of the cat that caused the election of Dick who was not even an alderman. Anne was rather relieved when the curtain fell and she could look over the balustrade to see if her father was sitting with Mrs Borrow. There was no sign of him and Mrs Borrow's seat was empty. At last, at the end of the interval, he reappeared. He ran down the circle steps in a jaunty way, smiling broadly and said: 'I'm sorry. I was talking to a friend.'

'I know,' said Anne, 'I saw you go out with a lady.'

'Oh!' Mr Jackson was silent for some moments, then, as the curtain rose on the last act, he said: 'Now, you'll enjoy this: "The Palace on the Night of the Grand Ball".'

The scene was all white, gold an silver, and Dick, in sky-blue satin tights, wearing a mayor's hat and chain of office, was a magnificent sight. The cat, dancing with a giant fish-bone, was funnier than ever, yet Anne could not enjoy it as she had enjoyed the first scene. Even at the end, when Gloria and Dick appeared in white satin as bride and groom, and silver tissues fell to transform the set, she could not feel as she had expected to feel when she was longing for the day of the pantomime to arrive. Then everyone on the stage was bowing; the house shook with applause, and she realized it was all over.

The street was dark when they went out but in the main road the shops, alight for the New Year, glittered in the icy air.

'What about tea?' Mr Jackson suggested.

Anne said sadly: 'Mummy said she'd expect us back for tea.'

'All right, then. Back we go.'

The sense of strain had returned between them. On the bus, Mr Jackson said in an embarrassed way: 'I wouldn't mention to your mother that I met that lady. She might think it odd.'

'I won't tell her,' Anne promised.

She was glad to get into the warm sitting-room where Marie was lying on the sofa, better now that it was too late. Mrs Jackson was making toast by the fire. There was some of the Christmas cake left and the decorations still hung round the fireplace. Here Anne was able to talk naturally about the pantomime and, forgetting Mrs Borrow, she mimicked the cat so well that Marie became weak with giggles.

Mr Jackson drank tea but would not eat anything. He had nothing to say, but when he put down his cup, he took off his shoes. It was wonderful – he was going to stay home that evening. As soon as he went upstairs to get his slippers and old jacket, Mrs Jackson gripped Anne's arm and whispered fiercely: 'He didn't go off and speak to anyone during the interval? I suppose you didn't see *her*?'

Anne gave her mother a startled look. She blushed painfully as she said: 'I don't think so.'

'Tell me at once,' Mrs Jackson's grip tightened: 'You wouldn't deceive me, would you, Anne? So she *was* there! I felt it. My instinct always tells me. No wonder he was so eager to take you children. He wouldn't do anything for you if he hadn't got something else in mind. And what happened? Did he go and sit with her? I suppose he told you to say nothing about it?'

'Well, there was a lady, but—'

'Ah-ha!'

'But it may have been a different lady.'

'A different lady!' Mrs Jackson echoed derisively; and added urgently: 'What were they doing?'

'They went to the bar. They were drinking wine.'

'*Wine!*' Mrs Jackson spoke the word as though wine were the very token of iniquity. She said no more but rose from her chair with the face of one who savours the delectation of betrayal. With her back to the fire, standing upright, her eyes very bright, she watched the door through which her husband would appear.

Frightened and helpless, Anne knew that nothing she could do or say would mend matters now. She could hear her father's old jaunty step as he came down the stairs and tears began to trickle down her cheeks. Her father was humming one of the pantomime songs as he came up the hallway and she felt deeply sorry for him.

Mrs Jackson's lips tightened. She waited until he had entered the room and closed the door before she said: 'Well!'

Their eyes met. Mr Jackson turned and looked at Anne.

'No wonder you were so keen to give the children a treat,' his wife jeered: 'No wonder you were suddenly so generous!'

'What have you been telling your mother?' Mr Jackson asked Anne.

'Nothing,' Anne sobbed.

Mrs Jackson broke in: 'Of course the child told me. Did you expect her to deceive her own mother?'

Mr Jackson went on staring at Anne who, lifting tear-filled eyes, saw he was both angry and hurt. She pleaded for understanding: 'Mummy asked me and—'

'And you told her! Well, now you see what you've done and I hope you're satisfied. I never thought you could be such a miserable little mischief-making sneak!' He made for the door.

His wife shouted after him: 'If she's a sneak, she takes after you.'

They heard him go upstairs again. Mrs Jackson breathed heavily, absorbed in her wrongs, taking no notice of Anne's tears. Marie had started to cry in sympathy. They could hear Mr Jackson moving about as he changed back into his out-door clothes, then he descended the stairs at a run and left the house, slamming the front door after him.

Mrs Jackson looked irritably at her weeping daughters: 'All right for him,' she said: 'He can get away. He can leave his troubles behind him.' During the evening she did not speak except once when she said again the word: 'Wine'. This time the note of disapproval had gone and in its place there was inquiry, even regret, as though it had occurred to her that somewhere, in a life which she had lived with such moral certainty and decision, there might have been something she had missed.

London, 1948.

The Incurable

The Incurable

As David Brady entered the hotel dining-room he glanced over the tables in an habitual search. He was not conscious of looking for anything, but as he looked he recognized his drop in expectation and was annoyed with himself that even now, in middle age, after fifteen years of marriage, the search went on. And what could he hope to find here in a town of elderly invalids? Only the girl in the corner had bothered to look up as he entered, and she, apparently engrossed in the talk of the old gentleman who shared her table, had looked away again at once.

A waiter intercepted him. David explained that he was not staying at the hotel – just taking his meals there.

'You are alone?' asked the waiter.

'My wife will be with me at the end of the week.'

The girl glanced up again at the sound of his voice and he found his second glimpse of her more promising. A pleasant oval face, no great beauty, of course, but the most remarkable eyes – light-coloured, a sort of silver-grey surrounded by black and heavy lashes that shadowed the whole eye-socket. 'Two holes in a blanket burnt through', as the song said. Taking his seat, he smiled to himself and his mood lightened. Not in anticipation. Oh no, he had no wish to explore beyond that hint of profundity. He was getting too old for all that.

Now he knew his life was settled and it was, in its way, satisfactory. The thing was merely that when he travelled alone he felt . . . well, not release exactly – that was too dramatic an idea and unfair to Barbara who gave him freedom enough – but the sort of infantile adventurousness he had felt on a summer day in childhood when, for the first time, he broke through the garden hedge into the world beyond. It had always seemed to him that somewhere, outside the routine of his life, there was to be found the quality of infinity. His search so far was a record of failure. As he thought that, he sighed and smiled at the same time, and found himself smiling at his own reflection in the mirror opposite. The reflection – still youthful, still handsome – smiled back with that mild air of sympathetic understanding which had too often involved him in relationships he had had no real intention of pursuing.

Before his soup arrived, the girl and the man finished their meal and passed his table on their way out of the room. The man, leaning on a stick, gave David a nod. David, when he nodded back, turned, in spite of himself, to the girl, but she was not looking at him. Well, what did it matter? He had intended no more than the contemplation of possibilities impossible to him.

That evening, entering the hotel before dinner, he glanced into the lounge and saw the girl sitting alone near the door. She was looking at a large, glossy periodical. She flicked the pages over, her eyes unfocused, and he could feel her boredom like an atmosphere about her. The old man, he supposed, was lying down or still at the Pump Room – but he was neither. Drifting into the bar, David saw him there, comfortably settled in with a double whisky in front of him.

They had the place to themselves and were soon in conversation. David gathered, during the careful to and fro of self-introductory remarks, that the old man was a Mr

Lennox, a widower: the girl, Ellie, his child of a late marriage. The two spent a lot of time at different spas. Mr Lennox had arthritis in one leg. He tapped his stick on the tiled floor in a wry, half-humorous indication that he was a cripple, but broke off with an 'enough of that' air. He might be afflicted, but he could still think of others.

'It's not much of a life for Ellie,' he said. 'Doesn't give her a chance to make friends. People arrive; you like the look of 'em; you get talking, but by the time you're on easy terms, off they have to go again. We say we'll meet again some time, but that's usually the end of it.' He paused to call another round from the barman before adding: 'Her mother died when Ellie was sixteen. Sad for a girl.'

It seemed to David that the situation was being presented to him in brief, almost with urgency, as though to the father it had recently taken on a quality of desperation.

'But she's still very young.'

'Nearly thirty.' Mr Lennox shook his head despondently, his eye upon the two glasses the barman was bringing round to them. He murmured as these were put on the table: 'Only drink I'm allowed.'

'She looks ten years younger,' said David.

Mr Lennox ignored this comment and continued his story. He seemed to be in the habit of telling it: 'But she's a good girl, a good girl. She says she's quite content with her old dad,' he drank complacently. ' 'Course it's not now that's the trouble; it's when I'm gone. That's why I feel I don't want to stand in her way.'

David made an appreciative sound and Mr Lennox, his point made, changed the subject abruptly: 'I used to be with Farquhar, Kist and James, the steel people.'

David made a show of interest, but he had no idea what sort of position this statement implied. He could only suppose

[177]

a man who spent most of the year in hotels of this sort was not a poor man. He responded by telling Mr Lennox that he kept a bookshop in Mayfair. The fact was his wife ran the shop. He specialized in rare and modern first editions and Barbara's competence left him free to visit provincial bookshops and country house auctions.

Mr Lennox, in his turn, showed interest, but when he spoke again a new, subtle note of patronage had come into his voice. He obviously saw David not as a person of some learning and culture, the friend (as he was) of collectors and men of letters, but as a small shopkeeper – not to be despised (no doubt Mr Lennox had started himself at the bottom of the ladder) but to be kept in his place. David, whose charm resulted partly from humility, smiled and wondered if this changed attitude would cancel the invitation to friendship implied in the earlier confidences. No, when the dinner-bell rang the old man, with a hint of condescension, said: 'We were thinking of running over to Cheselhunt tomorrow. Wonder if you'd care to join us?'

'Thank you. I certainly would,' said David, who had, in any case, intended to pay Cheselhunt a visit before Barbara arrived. Tomorrow a quick look over the local bookshops would decide him whether it would be worth while spending a night there.

When Mr Lennox and David came together into the dining-room, Ellie was already at the table. David expected from her some acknowledgment of the fact that he and her father had become acquainted, but she gave none. After dinner, David sat on at his table smoking slowly until the Lennoxes had left the room; he then went to the lounge. He had decided to try and get into conversation with Ellie. He wanted, of course, no more than a hint of the sort of woman that existed behind those eyes . . . He would be caution itself. Less than a month ago he had promised Barbara there would be no more emotional upsets. No more women would burst into the shop and, in front of customers, accuse her of holding David against his will. No more woman would . . . Oh, well, that was all in the past. He was, had always been, and would remain a contentedly married man.

He gave a glance into the bar; made sure that Mr Lennox was safely settled there, then, with an irrepressible twinge of excitement, hurried to the lounge. The girl was not there. He felt absurdly disappointed.

As he went out through the hall he asked the porter: 'Is Miss Lennox in?'

'Yes, sir. Just gone up to her room. Shall I ring through for you?'

'Oh, no, don't disturb her,' he said quickly, and he returned in a bleak mood to the flat that a friend had lent him.

Next day, directly after luncheon, Ellie brought the car round to the hotel entrance. Except for that first unrevealing stare, David had not had a glance from her. Now, when the old man introduced them, she gave a brief, non-committal smile but did not look directly at him.

Mr Lennox pointed with his stick at the seat next to her: 'You get in there, Brady. I like the back. Room for m'leg.'

At first, as they drove out through the smooth, sunlit, summer country, the old man talked and David sat askew in his seat to listen, but soon a sleepy silence settled on the back seat and David turned carefully, as though nervous of waking a child, and faced the front again. He said quietly, intimately: 'If ever you want a job as a chauffeur, I'll gladly employ you.'

She smiled but said nothing. It was, when he thought of it, not a particularly good opening – flirtatious without being funny; lending itself to response only by someone willing to carry on the flirtation.

When they parked in Cheselhunt market-place, David, discouraged, believing himself bored, took an expert look at the main bookshop, noted that its stock – large, but displayed without method – was promising, and decided to spend Thursday here, returning in time to meet Barbara's train on Friday evening.

As soon as he had seen Mr Lennox and Ellie settled in the chintz tea-room of the main hotel, he went to the desk to book a room. Once that was done, he felt relieved, as though he had planned an escape. A waiter had brought tea and Ellie started pouring it as soon as David returned. Watching the uncertainty of her movements, he thought that she might be thirty but, really, she was like an adolescent. He smiled at himself for being disturbed by her, and, with new confidence and detachment, took over the entertainment of the tea-table. He told several stories of visits to auctions in places like Cheselhunt where he had picked up valuable books for a few shillings each. When he described how he had once bought a bundle of books for half-a-crown and re-sold two of them for fifty guineas, the old man said with respect: 'Did you now!' and Ellie raised her head and fixed David with the full stare of her silver-coloured, dark-fringed eyes. Even at that moment her expression was oddly guarded, but it touched his nerves so, suddenly, he had nothing to say.

After a short silence, Mr Lennox spoke: 'Probably you young people want to get out and look around? Go on, the pair of you. I'll stay here and rest. Come back about six.'

Strolling out in the sunlit square, David reflected that, given an opportunity like this in the past, he had always talked easily and well; now he kept to the safety of silence. It was not that he had not meant what he had said to women in the past – with his temperament he always meant what he said, when he said it – but that now he felt whatever he said to this girl would sound premeditated, even false.

In the end she seemed driven to say something herself: 'I suppose you feel sorry for me.'

His quick glance showed him her up-tilted, cold profile; he answered with careful casualness: 'No, not particularly. Should I be?'

'Hasn't Daddy told you what a dismal life I lead? That I'm a poor creature who has failed to find a husband because we're always on the move?' As David opened his mouth to protest, she added: 'I know he did. He tells everybody that. He can't help it. He seems to have it on his mind; but he's wrong. I have quite a good life. I don't need to be pitied.'

David answered: 'I thought that myself. As soon as I saw you, I knew you were someone with . . . with great inner resources.'

She said nothing. He was uncertain whether or not he had reassured her until, meeting his worried glance, she burst out laughing. He realized her whole manner had changed. It was as though a misunderstanding had been cleared up between them and now she felt free to be herself. She stopped outside the bookshop and said: 'I suppose you want to go on a treasure hunt?'

'No important treasure here,' he said. 'These chaps know too much – but I might pick up a few firsts of someone like Henry James. No one is going to pay much for him here, but in Mayfair it's different.'

'Let's have a look.'

They went into the gloom of the shop and stood close together between shelves. Her hands moved nervously over the books and picked out one after another without looking at any of them. When she spoke she did so with a slightly breathless agitation: 'Look. Only a shilling! How much could you sell that for in Mayfair?'

'I don't expect I could sell it at all.' He watched her long, pallid hand push the book back, then pull out another. She was wearing a solitaire emerald that slipped from side to side as though her finger had shrunk away from it. At the dark end of the shop, when he slid past her, he touched her at the waist – an accident, as it were. She seemed not to notice, but she murmured with disappointment when the shopkeeper started closing his shutters.

'Better get back to the hotel,' said David, and he put a hand to her shoulder, propelling her out with an affectionate intimacy that made her cheeks glow.

'Now,' he thought, 'this must be the end of it,' and he turned in a businesslike way back to Mr Lennox. Going back in the car he gave the old man all his attention.

But that was not to be the end of it. The next day, after luncheon, Mr Lennox said he was going to lie down, but why didn't Ellie take Mr Brady for a run to Brentwood where there was an excellent bookshop? He spoke as though he expected David to jump at the suggestion.

Ellie, in an urgent half-whisper, said: 'Perhaps Mr Brady has other plans. He may not want to come.'

'But I do,' David said, and he was pleasantly beset by the sense of his own folly.

Something of his fears must have been conveyed to Ellie when they set out, and her manner became matter-of-fact, even off-hand, as though to reassure him. He was perhaps too easily reassured, for the atmosphere quickly relaxed between them and, talking of music, films, plays and books, they were delighted to find their tastes to be almost identical. Once or twice when David passed a judgment – not new but always intelligent – Ellie took her glance off the road and regarded him with so acute an appreciation he felt his resolution melting within him. On a long, uneventful stretch of road she let her left hand drop from the wheel to lie in the sunlight on the seat. He watched it until he felt forced to cover it with his own. Almost at once a car started to overtake them and she returned her hand to the wheel, but as she moved it from him she did so with the slowness of a caress.

Brentwood, when they reached it, looked an unpromising village. They left the car and went to look for the bookshop but could find only a newsagent who had a few paper-backs in his window.

'Isn't Daddy funny?' said Ellie. 'Why did he say there was a bookshop here? I don't believe he's ever been here.'

At the end of the village, beyond the last white cottage, stretched a meadow pollen-golden and aglitter with butter-cups. A path ran across it and disappeared into a clump of trees.

They climbed over the stile and, side by side, wandered towards the trees' shadow as towards a goal. When his swinging hand touched hers, her fingers caught and held to his. They walked in silence. As they passed into the cool and sudden darkness beneath the trees, they paused and moved towards each other. Her body sank against him and they kissed without a word. When at last he lifted his head and looked at her, her eyes, meeting his, were deep and luminous with a passion that startled him.

He took a step away from her and, already in retreat, put an arm round her waist and led her back into the sunlight, across the field to the road. He had noticed a teashop in the village and now brought her to it as though it offered adequate excuse for his return. As soon as they were settled in a corner, their order given, he said gently: 'I want to thank you.'

'For what?' she looked at him in surprise.

'For being kind. There are not many women who will give so much understanding to a married man.'

She said only: 'Are you unhappily married?'

After a reflective pause, he sighed: 'It would be unfair to say that. I am very fond of Barbara, in a way; I couldn't bear to hurt her. That's the trouble, of course. One gets trapped in a hopeless situation by one's own pity – but I think you understand that. I think you understand everything.'

She ate her tea without speaking. The silence of the homeward journey made David reflect uncomfortably that she probably understood too much. He was unwilling to fall in her estimation. When he spoke to her and she looked round to answer him, he was chilled by the casualness of her manner. It was she who had retreated now, and too far and too soon. He had intended nothing like that. There were, after all, degrees of safety, and he had hoped to achieve one more delicately nostalgic, regretful and poised for renewal of danger. Not that there could be any real question of renewal – yet! He was troubled in spite of himself by the recollection of her emotion beneath the trees. There, surely, he had glimpsed what he had been seeking all his life! And must she, because he was not free to respond, shut herself so completely away from him?

When the silence had gone on too long, he said: 'Tell me you're not cross with me.'

'Cross with you!' she echoed, surprised again – and he could do nothing but sigh.

When they reached the hotel, he said he would go round with her to the garage. They walked back in the sunset light, their day nearly at an end – but there was no change in her manner. She seemed scarcely aware of him. In the hall, as she moved towards the lift, he caught her elbow and said: 'No, come up the stairs.' She went, no doubt to avoid a scene of

[184]

any sort. Alone at last, in the shadows of the first-floor landing, he stood in front of her, holding her elbows and gazing down intently at her while she looked away.

He said: 'You know I love you.'

She did not reply, but now she looked at him. As she met his steady, adoring stare, the suspicion passed from her eyes; they grew tender, grew a little moist; then she broke away, murmuring: 'Tomorrow.'

He held to her hand: 'Tomorrow I have to go to Cheselhunt, but I'll be back on Friday.' He kissed the back of her fingers and whispered: 'So beautiful and so kind,' but she pulled her hand away and ran into her room.

He went off next morning on an early bus. He was in a pleasant mood, conscious of the situation left unresolved behind him and relieved that he was putting himself beyond the reach of its temptation. His abstinence, because it was of his own choosing, gave him a rare sense of self-sufficiency, so all the time he was alone in Cheselhunt he felt released and independent. Perhaps because of this he forgot the times of the return buses next evening and so missed the one that would have enabled him to meet Barbara's train. He did not worry much. She had no key to the flat but she knew he was eating at the hotel; she would wait for him there. It was nearly ten before he got back and Barbara, as he had expected, was in the lounge. He looked round quickly and, thankful that Ellie was not about, crossed, smiling, to his wife.

'Well, there you are!' she said, unconcerned, accepting him almost without looking at him. He began to apologize for being late, but she cut him short with: 'Oh, I guessed something had held you up,' and rose to go with him. She looked pallid, tired and strained by her London indoor life.

'Where's your bag?' he asked.

'In the hall. I'll see you there. I've left some things in the cloakroom.'

While he stood waiting in the hall, Ellie came down the stairs with some letters in her hand. She gave a cry on seeing him and ran towards him, her hands out, her face alight . . . He whispered a warning and appeal: 'My wife is here.'

'Oh!' She stiffened at once. She stood a moment, looking at the letters in her hand, then, on an impulse, handed him one of them. The others she threw on the porter's table and, instantly turning, she disappeared upstairs.

The letter she had given him was addressed to him here at the hotel. He opened it, drew out a sheet of hotel paper and, reading rapidly, received from her words not so much their meaning as an excitement that transported him beyond the trivialities of the present. He saw himself escaping with this girl to some warm and brilliant country – he did not know where, but a country beyond the importunings of a world in which he had always felt in the wrong. For a visionary moment he was already out of reach of his own consciousness of failure, of Barbara's irrepressible rightness and of all the responsibilities that narrowed his life into the commonplace. It was as though his feet had already left the ground. He was turned towards the stairs, on the point of running up to Ellie's room, throwing open her door and calling to her 'Come!' – she would know where and to what future – when Barbara came into the hall. When she saw him she started to grumble about some trouble over cloakroom tickets. He slid Ellie's letter into his side-pocket. Her eyes followed his movement but did not seem to take it in. She pushed her coat at him. He held it for her to put on, not listening to the cloak-room-ticket story but, as best he could from his retreat into the remotest regions of fancy, responding to it with an indignant grunt or two.

'Do tuck my collar down properly,' she said, carrying her irritation over to him.

He did what she told him. Her voice, as familiar as their bedroom furniture, broke into his dream, firmly displacing it until, with bitterness, tedium and relief, he felt his own senses adjust themselves to familiar ground.

In the depression that now flooded over him, he moved ahead of her as though to get away from her. Thus, in the porch, she was able to slide two fingers into his pocket and draw out the letter. Too late, he clapped his hand down to stop her. He said angrily, but without hope of being obeyed: 'Give that back.' He might have tried to snatch it had not the porter come into the hall and looked at them through the glass of the door. She, indifferent to the porter, stood under the porch light and read the letter. David moved wretchedly into the outer darkness. Having glanced once over the page, she read it aloud, her voice null with the nullity of someone who has passed beyond even a sense of long-suffering:

'I have longed for you. I have eaten nothing since I left you. I have wandered about, dazed with love, longing only to see you again. Everything that has come between me and my memory of you, has filled me with impatience. Whenever I have looked away from the things about me, I have seen your face. I think I have been waiting for you since the day I was born. And yet you accuse me of kindness.'

Barbara paused before she read the signature, then pronounced it with a certain pathos: ' "Ellie". This poor girl, whoever she is, is in love with you.'

David shrugged his shoulders, glad the accusation was no worse. 'Well, what can one do about it?' He started to move off, on edge to get away from the hotel.

Barbara following after him, asked wearily: 'I suppose you're not in love with her?'

He said from habit: 'Don't be silly,' and she, from habit, took this as denial.

'You're incurable.' She looked at the letter again and said: 'She's staying at the hotel. Well, we'd better not go in there again. There are plenty of other places where we can get a meal,' and she carefully tore the paper into small pieces. These she held until they came to a dustbin someone had put outside a front door. She stopped, lifted the lid and tucked the pieces down among the refuse.

David watched her, aware that her attitude in doing this was not, as it had often been in the past, one of anger or contempt, but only of dispassionate good sense. He recognized the justice of adopting this attitude towards him, the incurable romantic, and yet even as he did so he hated her as though she had wantonly taken from him and destroyed his sanction to pass through a door which must now be closed against him for ever.

London, 1951.

The Guillemot

The Guillemot

When the train reached Ferrel there were only nine people left on it. Eight of these alighted at once and made off confidently. They had reached home. Pulling herself together, Isabel stepped down to the platform and looked about her. There had been no conversation on the train, no introduction to this strange county. The glances she met had been self-absorbed or suspicious. At any other time they would have disturbed her, now, of course, she did not care.

From here she had to find her way to Salem Minor and the bay. Edward's secretary, Miss Plumtree, had told her there was a bus from Ferrel to Salem Minor. While receiving these instructions, at luncheon in the Fleet Street A.B.C., Isabel had wept. Perhaps it had been unfair to let Miss Plumtree guess, at this late hour, what Isabel had promised to keep secret, but she could not restrain herself. She was in a sort of exaltation of grief. She had felt, she had to admit, a certain comfort in betraying herself. Later she had felt ashamed – the dead cannot come to their own defence – and despair had taken the place of her exaltation. It seemed that only then she had realized how hopelessly dead Edward was.

In London, Ferrel and Salem Minor and the bay had been so remote, she imagined that by journeying to them, she must journey into a different state of mind. But here she was at Ferrel and despair had come with her.

She spoke to the ticket-collector. He was as discouraging as the rest of them but he directed her to the bus stop on the road above. As she made her way up wooden steps, between bramble bushes, she felt no foreign country could be less friendly than this. The thought made her aware of the temerity of her undertaking, and the cost. She had travelled overnight to Bodmin and had hoped to return there to catch the night train back. Now she realized she could never do it in the time. She would have to pay for a bed somewhere, and buy food for the next day's journey. Whatever happened, she had to be back at her office on Monday morning.

For many weeks she had been lifted by sorrow above the circumstances of daily life. Nothing had worried her, neither the irritants of the present nor the precariousness of the future. Now, it seemed, worry was breaking in on her again. Her first sense of purpose had lost its impetus. She realized there had been something crazy in setting out, with only two free days, to see this bay – the bay Edward had loved in childhood and where he had asked for his ashes to be scattered. Perhaps she had become a little crazy since he died.

While waiting for the bus she bought a sandwich at a milk-bar. The sandwich was wrapped in transparent paper, but it was dry; it contained a very thin, small piece of ham. As she ate, she gazed over the cliff-edge rail and saw the Ferrel shore spread below, shaped and coloured like an oyster-shell, and lit, on that winter noon, with a salt-white light that made space more spacious. Breathing the bland and humid air, she felt uplifted again, justified in setting out on any pilgrimage that could return her to contact with Edward.

The bus took her inland. Here the scene was disappointing. The country was flat and colourless, sparsely grassed, with stones appearing in the fields. There was some beauty in the distances, softened by mist as by a touch of powder, but the whole area was littered with army debris. Camps of black huts stood weathering into squalor, the barbed-wire about them red with rust. One airfield was still in use. A large jet aircraft shot over the bus with such force some of the passengers ducked their heads. By the roadside two aircraftmen stood trying to thumb a lift in the other direction.

The villages were slate-grey beneath a grey sky. When Edward had talked of Cornwall, Isabel had imagined something very different from this.

The bus stopped at the end of a lane. The driver told her that a few hundred yards down the lane she would come to a cliff-edge and see Salem Minor below. In the air there was a half-mist, smelling of the sea. She unrolled her raincoat and put it on.

The lane, overhung with trees, dropped steeply, stony and marked by miniature streams, till it reached a natural platform on the cliff verge. Some rocks had been placed there to form a seat. She sat for a while and gazed over the V-shaped valley down each flank of which houses trickled like sugar lumps into folded paper. They had accumulated at the bottom of the valley, where they faced a delicately inwashing, grey-green sea.

The mist was clearing. The sinking sun, breaking through, polished the damp air. A house, spot-lit on the opposite cliff-top, gleamed terracotta. The rest of the village was coldly in shadow, but beyond the shadow the sea, newly lit, had taken on the colour of a blue scabious flower. The shore was packed with boats, all black-tarred, hung here and there with wine-coloured nets. Two men sat on the sea-wall. They were the only human beings in sight.

She continued down the rain-wet slope, passing among houses, until she reached the road below. The men on the wall must have heard her step but they did not glance round. She broke in on their silence to ask direction. After a pause so long she feared they would not speak at all, one of them grudgingly took the pipe from his mouth and pointed across the town to the path that climbed the opposite cliff. The bay, he said, was a mile or so along the shore.

As she passed down the main street she saw only one person, a woman who peered at her from a window with an air of enmity. Well, what did she care! Like the rest of the world, this place had no substance for her. Reality for her was in the company of the dead.

When she reached the cliff-top beyond the village, she could view the shore until it turned, in the distance, in a crescent of sand. That must be Edward's bay. At last she was in his country. The path carried her down again among rough grass, grey and heavy with rain, that grew between the sand and the stone wall of the fields.

Now, nearing her goal, she was so full of consciousness of Edward, it seemed to her at any moment she might come face-to-face with him. She mounted the brow of each slope, turned each corner, almost believing it must bring him into sight. She put out her hand to him, feeling him like a tangible presence, and said 'Edward' and looked about her, but she was alone. During the whole walk, she met no one.

The rain was drifting down again. As the clouds thickened, the blue tinge went from the sea. She preferred the gloom. She would have resented a day of full sunlight.

The last time she had seen Edward it had been a day like this, an autumnal Saturday of grey fine rain. He had suggested on the telephone they should drive to Marlow and have tea by the river there, but the day being what it was, he arrived at the meeting-place on foot. The car, he said, was not going well. He had left it in a garage. He apologized for disappointing her. She said 'I don't mind what we do. I only want to be with you.'

He had smiled and squeezed her hand. She had said that so

often he did not now bother to protest. For eight years they had been meeting like this, once or twice a week, and at first he used to say: 'My dear, you must not waste your life on me. You know nothing can come of it. You must find yourself some nice young man and marry and be happy,' and she had always replied she could be happy with no one but him. If he had made the break and refused to see her, perhaps by now she would have found someone else. She was not a plain girl or lacking in vivacity. Contemplating an empty future, she wondered if there was still time – then she put the thought behind her. She had been faithful to Edward. She would remain faithful to Edward. At their first meeting she had told herself: 'This is the man I want,' and even after the early excitement of their relationship had faded, she had held to him as the only one she wanted. She had held obstinately. She had refused to consider the possibility of anyone else, even when she realized he had never had any real intention of breaking his marriage. If she were foolish enough to let things drift on through the years – demanding nothing, in a position to demand nothing – then he was not the one to stop it. She had been aware of her own unwisdom, and gloried in it. She was staking all on the thing she wanted. At the back of her mind there was always the knowledge that Hilda was a semi-invalid, a frail creature, tubercular. Isabel might win him in the end.

Over the years, by cautious telephone calls, by disguised visits to Edward's office, she had come to know Miss Plumtree. Occasionally, lunching in the same restaurants, they had shared a table. Miss Plumtree was a middle-aged woman who saw herself as an eternal girl. If she suspected Isabel's relationship with Edward, she never showed suspicion, but once or twice she made, with a giggle, remarks that stabbed Isabel to the heart. Not long before Edward's death, she had said: 'A little bird tells me the boss is too friendly with someone he's not married to. I think I know who it is.'

'Who?' Isabel breathlessly asked.

'Ah!' Miss Plumtree smirked down at her plate for some moments before she said: 'A very charming widow lady who has been ringing him up rather a lot lately.'

Isabel, who had grown hot with fear at what might be revealed, then grew cold and it was some time before she had the heart to speak again.

Another time, Miss Plumtree, with sniffs and down-turnings of the lips, had hinted her dislike of Edward's wife, Hilda.

'A grizzler, I'd call her,' said Miss Plumtree.

Isabel took this opportunity to ask: 'Do you think he'll ever leave her?'

Miss Plumtree's eyes opened and she fixed Isabel with a knowing look. What it was she knew Isabel did not dare to guess. Looking away and pursing her lips, she tormented Isabel with silence for a while, then said: 'Not him. They understand each other, those two. They'll never separate.'

It was then, for the first time, Isabel knew she wanted Hilda to die. But it was Edward who died.

That last wet autumn afternoon when they met, they decided to go to a cinema. The film they wanted to see, one they had missed at the central cinemas, had reached the Elephant and Castle. They went into the Green Park underground station. On the train, she saw him puzzling over the railway map opposite him.

He turned to her, shaking his head slightly, and said with an impatience she had hardly ever known in him before: 'I don't know. I can't make it out.'

She looked at the map and saw at once that they must change at Piccadilly Circus for the Bakerloo Line: 'Edward darling,' she said, 'your brain is going to sleep.'

He answered her seriously: 'At times, that's what it seems like.' His tone made her look at him. She saw him staring in a hurt, bewildered way straight before him. She slipped her fingers into his hand and leant against him and whispered: 'What is the matter?'

He turned quickly and laughed at her: 'Nothing, silly.'

But there was something the matter. He had been examined during the past week and declared in perfect health. It was not until a few days after their last meeting that the brain specialist had diagnosed the abscess which was killing him. He had collapsed suddenly after that. He had not returned to his office. Isabel had never heard from him again. She had telephoned several times and asked for him in what she hoped was a disguised voice, and been told he was away ill. She passed through a month of frantic anxiety before she could bring herself to ask the truth from Miss Plumtree.

'But can't they operate?' she had cried over the telephone.

'I am sure,' Miss Plumtree had said impatiently, 'everything that can be done, is being done.'

Miss Plumtree, no doubt, was worried about her own position, and with reason. It was not so easy to get another job when one was fifty.

Miss Plumtree was Isabel's only source of news. She and Edward had had no friends in common. They had met by accident in the years just after the war when taxi-cabs were scarce and several people shared them. She and Edward, reaching the head of the queue together at King's Cross, had driven together to Bloomsbury, conversing pleasantly. She had felt no surprise when she found he was a free-lance journalist with an office a few hundred yards from that in which she worked, for she felt she knew him, had always known him and would know him for ever. A few days later they had come face-to-face in the Strand and he had asked her to take tea with him. So it had begun, to last . . .

'For ever,' she said, 'for ever,' transported by this thought so she scarcely noticed the strange and lonely shore she was traversing.

The path had faded out into sandy grass. She became aware that her feet were sinking deeper at every step. She moved down to the firm sand near the sea.

The sky was becoming dark. She passed the rusted remains of some sort of ship bedded well down into the sand. Rusted metal objects washed in with the ship lay half-buried at intervals along the shore. Beyond these the rocks started. On a headland of rock, at the sea edge, stood a group of tarred wooden buildings, dilapidated and deserted, the windows boarded up. A door creaked ajar. She looked inside and saw machinery standing in the shadows.

This sign of past human occupation disturbed her more than the solitude. It enhanced the silence and desertion of the place, and the wildness of the brambled headland she had now to cross. Everything was pearled with rain. Her shoes were soaking. Reality, with its cold and discomfort, broke into her dream state.

At last, through the brambles, she saw the gleam of sand again. This must be Edward's bay. At the edge of the headland, looking down, she saw the sea below, misted so it looked like green milk. It was moving delicately, casting out on the sand and drawing back again small nets of foam. Here it was easier to understand why Edward loved the place.

She climbed down the rocks to the bay. In its winter desertion, it might have been the shore of an uninhabited island. The light was beginning to fail. She knew she must not stay long – but she had arrived. Here, if anywhere, Edward must now be.

She would walk a little way along the sand. Within the first fifty yards, she came on the body of a sea-bird, dead from no apparent cause, lying on its side at the water's edge. It was still unmarred by death, its plumage beautifully sleek in its marbling of black and white.

The word 'guillemot' came into her head. She had forgotten she had ever known it. In her childhood, when taken on holiday to the seaside, her father, the source of all knowledge then, had told her the names of sea-birds. He had grown up on the Isle of Wight. When he was a boy, he said, there had been great settlements of guillemots on the island's cliffs. Every breeding season men 'calling themselves "sportsmen" ', her father had given an angry emphasis to the word, had visited the island with guns and slaughtered the birds, leaving the bodies to be washed away by the sea – slaughtered them ruthlessly and irresponsibly, so the nestlings starved to death and, in the end, the settlements were wiped out. His indignation at this savage and useless 'sport' had been conveyed to her. She felt it again now – a fury, a need to fight, but she did not know what to fight. Her eyes filled with tears. She felt a scarcely bearable pain of loss and her tears streamed down her face.

She suffered for the guillemot as she suffered for Edward, so needlessly dead, wiped out while his body was still young and unspoilt. At the end he must have looked, like the guillemot, dead without cause.

As she turned to walk back again, she felt the wind cold in her face. She paused at the dead bird and gave it a last look. The sea was touching it now, washing gently between the feathers and the sand, lifting the body a little. Soon it would be carried out to sea. Only she would know it had ever been there.

She walked on. Only she now knew of her years with Edward. If she were to speak of them, people would think she was building a romance out of nothing. When she died their relationship, which had taken her youth, had filled her life so no other thing or person had mattered, would be lost without trace.

She climbed the rocks and paused again, to look back over the bay. From here its vast incurve looked like a shark's mouth, a mile or more from point to point. She thought of Edward's wife, small and solitary on this expanse of shore, scattering the ashes, and the wind carrying them away so they were lost, not even a little dust on the sand, but dispersed into nothingness.

Already, she realized, her memory of Edward had moved a pace into the past. The sea of time was washing in about him. She felt the helplessness of the dead carried away into oblivion.

It roused a sudden revolt in her. She was not helpless yet. She was still alive.

The bay was bleak and wintry and indifferent as death. What had brought her here? She would not find Edward here. She would not find him anywhere. In the gloom of this twilight, the past, that had seemed to her her only reality, took on a quality of fantasy. The years behind her had no more substance than a dream. Perhaps she had imagined the whole relationship.

She began to hurry back to Salem Minor. She left behind the buildings with their rusting machinery, she left the buried ship and reached the path in the grass verge. There she ran till she reached the cliff-top from where she saw the lights of the village. The boats were clotted together at the dark verge of the sea. She hurried thankfully down until she was among the houses feeling like one who, long condemned to inhabit a region of phantoms, was at last returning to the living world.

London, 1953.

The End of the Street

The End of the Street

The Partridges, Marion and Peter, were driving into Hertfordshire to stay with her parents. They had left their Kensington flat at the first fall of the smoky winter twilight and had now reached the 'garden city' of Denton where rates were said to be low in order to attract industry.

Every time the young Partridges made this journey the white, box-like factories of Denton had eaten up a little more of the countryside. The town was no longer new. With the years it was becoming grimy and the once ultra-modern factory buildings were out-of-date, but the place still had a look of rootless immaturity. The trees planted down the roads to effect the 'garden' idea were at an uninteresting, untidy age. Behind them the red suburban houses were as raw as tomato ketchup.

Marion had always hated the place. The first roads had been laid out before the war, making a muddy blot among the Hertfordshire fields. She had been a child then and when she heard the grown-ups speak of the coming 'garden city' with derision and contempt, she knew she was right to hate it. It had not, as every one hoped, proved a financial failure. Every time she saw it, she felt affronted by its growth.

Peter, a manufacturer of ready-made men's wear, who had brought energy and ambition into his father's fine old business, had no idea that Marion felt this way about Denton. Himself, he thought it 'an up-and-coming town', nicely laid out and an asset to the county. Indeed, he was thinking of extending his own company by taking over a hosiery factory that was for sale in Denton. The owner had died in early middle age and the son, who wanted to be a writer or something, was willing to sell out at a bargain price. Peter had the keys in his pocket. He intended a quick look-round the layout. The surveyors, of course, would report on the structure and the accountants would go through the books with a fine toothcomb. Between them, they would probably be able to knock down the price.

He turned off from the main road and scouted through the back streets, looking out for the 'For Sale' notice. When it appeared, he drove the car on to a patch of ground beside the building. He told Marion he would not be five minutes. The car was an open vintage Daracq but it had been fitted with a heater that kept the front seat comfortable. Peter left the engine running so that Marion would not feel cold.

The owner had been ill a year before he died and it was evident that in that time no one had bothered about the factory surround that might once have been a garden and was now a rubbish dump.

'What a dismal place,' said Marion.

'We'll change all that,' Peter said as he went off.

A high wind was tossing the street-lights that were strung on wires across the road. Shadows dodged about over buildings in which, it seemed, life was not so much absent as extinct. A sense of desolation came down on Marion. Muffled in a fur coat and fur hood, wrapped in rugs, the heater sending its heavy warmth up round her legs, Marion felt a chill that did not come from the wind or the frosty December air.

She was, as she would tell people, a natural Londoner. As soon as she was old enough, she had found herself a job in London. She was not gregarious but she liked the sense that life was at hand. People, theatres, lighted streets, shop-windows – in the city these pleasures awaited one, so one could stay at home with a tranquil mind. She would, if she could, have had all the shops open on Sunday; not because she wanted to buy things on Sunday but because she could not bear that day of outside inactivity. When she was a country child, perhaps she did not notice the emptiness of small towns, but now it depressed her. She hated the dark-ness at the end of the street. The sense of desertion was a threat, related to something sinister but unidentified, met, perhaps, in dreams. At this thought, she was struck suddenly with the certainty that she had known this empty Denton street in another dimension. She had known it when she was disembodied, asleep or dead. This dejected loneliness was the loneliness of death. She was so appalled by this fantasy, that she was afraid. She looked round for Peter, as though she had been exiled by death into this solitude and would remain here for ever – then she heard the slam of the factory door. In a moment he was coming at a jog-trot over the waste-land, saying with concern: 'You haven't felt cold, have you? I haven't been long, have I?', his round, good-tempered, boyish face so drawn with concern that she burst out laugh-ing. The vision of herself as a solitary ghost wandering empty streets was gone in a moment. He took his seat in the car and slipping off her fur gloves, he rubbed her fingers between his big, warm, square hands. Certain of his adoring love, she felt so protected and secure she forgot that she would ever have to die at all.

When they returned to open country, the wind howled over their heads and whipped round their ears like a frozen towel.

As both were hatless, the back draught blew their hair forward into their eyes. Pushing her hair impatiently back, Marion said: 'Open the windscreen. Do open the windscreen.'

'Certainly not,' Peter pretended to be stern.

'Oh, do!' she wheedled him in a sweet little voice like a charming child.

He glanced down at her, protectively hesitant: 'But you will freeze. I can't have my baby dying of cold.'

The mention of death disturbed her so that she became impatient and said with a petulance that brooked no refusal: 'I want it open.'

He smiled indulgently and unscrewed the butterfly nuts. He pushed the screen open and the air rushed in like a dash of icy water in the face. She caught her breath, stunned by the wind and nestled down among her furs and scarves and rugs so only the tip of her nose was visible.

'Warmth, warmth,' she thought, yet she was excited by this painful cold. Peter gave her occasional sidelong glances, adoring and amused, as she crouched beside him sheltering from a blast that could, if she commanded, be shut out in a few seconds. But she did not command it, though her face was rigid as though a mask of ice had formed over it. With the wind blowing her eyelashes down into her eyes, she peered to see the Hertfordshire fields that were all much alike: large, flat and bordered with low hedges. In one the iron ground was patched with barley stubble; in another were enormous haystacks, stolid cone-shapes, black against the sky that had been blown clear by the wind. A gibbous moon suddenly appeared. Marion, the Londoner, sat up with surprise. She had not known there was a moon just then. The moon, that seemed to be hanging the wrong way round, threw a bleak unnatural light over the monotonous fields. She associated the word 'gibbous' with the word 'gibbet' and it occurred to her that this was a hangman's moon. The country looked desolate. She shuddered.

'Hey!' said Peter, 'we can't have this,' and he put out his hand to close the screen.

'No, don't,' she said and he laughed at her. He had never known such a woman. Everything she did and said charmed him with its originality, and, often enough, absurdity. He knew he was only an ordinary fellow and he could no more conceive an original remark than he could fly.

Marion sat close to him, feeling the warmth of his body. He was one of those people who never felt the cold. Even now, driving in the open Daracq, he did not wear a greatcoat. Sturdy and young, he sat upright at the wheel. With wide shoulders and a thick neck supporting a round, broad head, he did not look much like a successful businessman. He was rather indifferent about his clothes so that strangers were often surprised when they heard for the first time his light, cultured voice. He might have been a farmer. His face, with its prominent nose and wide straight mouth, had strength and an unimaginative intelligence.

When she caught his small, smiling eyes giving her one of his oblique glances, she reflected upon his blind adoration that she had accepted as she might accept an umbrella in a storm. She was grateful; she was fond of him, but she had always had in mind someone quite different. When she left home and went to London, she had imagined she would meet someone very like herself: sensitive, quick-witted, in some way remarkable – an artist, perhaps. The men of that sort whom she met did not seem to have marriage in mind. When she met Peter, she was excited by his difference as now she was excited by the rough wind. She could say what she liked to him and he was delighted. He never puzzled over her. To other people she could seem strange and difficult. She never felt quite confident of her reception in society and she was conscious of being misunderstood. But she was not strange to Peter. He was innocent of the quality of strangeness in things. Yet she was never quite sure whether her enchantment for him was that of an idol or a talking doll.

Her parents were almost shocked when she brought him home. They had expected much worse from Marion. How had she managed to captivate this normal, acceptable, wealthy young man?

Her mother had asked from curiosity what she saw in him. She answered casually that she found him physically attractive.

'But is that all?' her mother asked.

'Of course not,' she answered abruptly to discourage further questions. She felt rather irritated by their surprise and curiosity.

The truth was that, in spite of her verve and wit, she had not had much success in London. And she could not pretend that she had lacked opportunity. She had explained the situation when writing in her diary: 'How is it when I meet those intellectual explorers of the mind and the imagination that should be by rights my companions, I interest them only for a short time? They are attracted to me as to an undiscovered country, then they are disconcerted and wonder why they make no progress. As I continue to evade them, they begin to feel the futility of pursuit. They find me amorphous, bewildering, protean. In the end their enthusiasm dies, they become resentful and begin to dislike me. I have decided that only physical contact is possible and possible with someone like Peter Partridge who makes no attempt to understand me, who does not even wonder if I need understanding. I am thinking of marrying him.'

She was pleased and satisfied by this analysis of a situation that had begun to disturb her. Her analysis reconciled her to the fact that Peter was such an ordinary young man. She saw the wisdom of marrying him. Once married, she found she enjoyed the comforts that money could buy. Her marriage was like a warm, unquestioning bed in which she forgot the difficulties of the daytime. She wanted nothing more. She had, she decided, become mentally self-sufficient and only the physical need remained to be satisfied.

In sudden consciousness of satisfaction, she moved against him and he put his arm round her and drove with only one hand on the wheel. He could feel the thin, nervous line of her shoulder through the wraps he had heaped on her and he was stirred. She was a tiny creature, vital and quick-moving. He described her to himself as a little flame that dazzled him. But she was, of course, more than that. His honesty demanded a fundamental honesty in others and he felt it to be in her.

He had never understood his mother's distrust of Marion. When he took her home, his mother had said: 'Peter, I don't like that girl. There's something about her. Don't see too much of her, darling,' and Peter had been upset. He had once adored his mother exactly as he now adored Marion; and he saw her dislike of the girl as mortification at the sight of a rival. He had not thought seriously of marriage before; now he realized he had become a man and he needed a wife more than he needed a mother. His mother simply had to recognize that. He had given her his devotion for nearly thirty years and she had taken it as a right. She knew he was a man who had to give all his affection, all his allegiance unstintingly to one person. She was afraid that when he transferred his allegiance, there would be nothing left for her. Perhaps she had been right. Marion had devoured him. Her response, her physical delight in his passion, his faith in her as the completely right, the only possible person for him – these things had devoured him. Heavens, how he loved being devoured by her. He saw the union as a total one, a mystical concurrence of body, mind and soul.

When all this worship came to her, Marion did not take it unquestioningly. She was much too intelligent for that. She never ceased to uphold his belief in their conjunction as something fore-ordained since time began. What he gave she took with gratitude. She too believed in their union. She saw her past relationships as empty and pretentious. Peter had restored her to honesty. Yes, she was exactly what he believed her to be. She would never look at anyone else. She would never fail him by as much as a glance.

The marriage, now three years old, had been perfect. His mother's sad, forsaken face did not trouble him. Even her death a few months ago had not disturbed him very much. It was like the death of a deposed ruler: unimportant. Now that Marion was all things to him, he was content.

He caressed her cheek with his forefinger. She caught his hand and held it against her cheek. She turned her face and pressed her lips into the warm centre of his palm. She felt a deep consciousness of his love and the security he gave. She was content. Yes, amazingly, she was content. Her eyes filled with tears. She thrust her face into his jacket and slipped her arm across his waist.

'Darling Peter,' she whispered and he held her the tighter in understanding. An idealist and a believer, he was convinced he had found a flawless relationship that could survive the grave.

They were passing the first cottages of the village. The wind whirred here like an electric force through which the young couple made their way of a separate volition, safely apart and inseparable.

Now they had reached the drive into her father's vicarage. Peter swung the car round and they saw the garage doors standing open, waiting for their arrival. Peter turned the car round the small circular lawn in front of the house and backed it into the garage and shut off the engine. For some minutes he and Marion sat in silence and darkness, wrapped in a close embrace, unwilling to separate, unwilling to move out into an inhabited world where they would have to reveal themselves and take on individual identities. Beyond their own quiet they could hear the trees humming and quivering in the wind. They were old trees, looking, in their winter nakedness, as though they were growing roots upwards. Here and there among the branches could be seen the black smudge of a forgotten nest. Ragged, transparent cloud raced across the sky so the moon seemed in flight while remaining fixed in the sky.

Marion moved first. Becoming aware of the strange bleak light of the moon on the garden just beyond their darkness, she was disturbed and sat upright.

She said: 'They must have heard the car. We should go in.'

While he felt about on the back seat for the rug to put over the bonnet, she wandered out and stood alone in the drive. She could remember when the garage had been a stable and the manger was still fixed to the wall at the back. Old harness used to hang there on hooks, but Peter had improved it all. His was the car that changed the stables into a garage. As soon as he began to come here regularly, he had asked permission to move the manger that took up too much room and he had made a bonfire and burnt the old, dried-out, broken harness.

Marion watched him now as he lit two lamps and stood them on either side of the radiator of the vintage Daracq. She was a little jealous of this car to which Peter gave his spare time – not that he had much spare time when Marion took up so much of his life – and which she described as 'the interesting invalid'. She sometimes thought of asking him to sell the Daracq and buy a modern car, but her instinct told her that the Daracq was a better ritual object than most for draining off Peter's excess piety. Let him keep it. Besides, she liked driving in the open, in the penetrating cold, like a spoilt little Russian princess in a sleigh.

Now Peter was wrapping the old rug over the radiator. He was very thorough. He would leave nothing undone, even though she was waiting for him. He closed the doors and bolted them and then, at last came to her. He put an arm round her waist to lead her over the frozen, glimmering grass.

'No.' She did not want to go yet. She remained a little stiff and apart from him, and to excuse herself she said, 'Look.' She nodded towards the house front where the shadows moved as the wind bowed the larches one way and another. The vicarage was a Georgian house with thirteen long windows regularly placed in two rows upon its façade. Now almost all the windows were lit in welcome. Through three on the left of the portico could be seen Marion's father and brother decorating a Christmas tree. The brother was at the top of a step-ladder fitting on to the higher branches the brilliant objects which his mother was handing up to him. The father was appearing and disappearing as he went round the tree festooning it with glittering strands of tufted stuff. As they worked, they talked and laughed and made gestures, but no sound came out to the two standing on the frozen lawn. On the other side of the portico was the dining-room where a maid moved about a table laid for the expected guests. In the window above the portico the brother's wife talked to someone as she put her two children to bed.

Peter saw no reason for standing outside when a step or

two would take them into the heart of all this luminous activity: 'Come on, sweet,' he said, 'you don't want to catch cold.'

'Just a moment. Don't you love standing apart like this and looking in at other people living their lives? It's like being dead and watching the living doing things that you used to do yourself.'

The thought that had chilled her at Denton had now become entertainment. With so much love about her, it excited her to play with the old nightmares of loneliness and death. As Peter took her arm to persuade her indoors, she stepped away from him, insisting upon her isolation, and for the first time since their marriage, he found himself troubled by her. He, too, began to think of death and he realized that she, delicate creature that she was, might die first and leave him to suffer on for years without her. In all those years, she might drift away and get lost so he could never find her again.

He took hold of her urgently and said: 'If you die first, you will wait for me, won't you?'

She answered vaguely, become perverse with the sense of a doom upon her: 'If I can. But who knows what happens when one dies?'

He said: 'Wherever you go, I will find you.'

She looked at him, laughing, her expression so odd that she seemed a stranger, and said: 'Do you think you could recognize me without my body?'

It was only a chance remark, a joke really, and in a second the mood had passed and she forgot what she had said. But Peter could not forget. All that evening, at the jolly dinner-table, it remained like a hurt at the back of his mind. For weeks afterwards he brooded upon it, not understanding it until, suddenly, like a terrible revelation, its import swept over him. Then he thought of his mother's death as though it had happened only the day before. Regret settled into him. He began to believe he had exchanged his mother's love for a transient and worthless illusion. He became haunted by a sense of loss.

Marion, worried, asked herself what had occurred to make him so abstracted. She began telling their acquaintances that all men were alike: as soon as you gave them all they wanted, they began seeking diversion. Peter, with the memory of his mother's face in his mind, began searching the faces of the women he met. It seemed to him that if he looked long enough, he would find that sad, forsaken face somewhere again.

London, 1935. Rewritten, 1963.

A Romantic Hero

A Romantic Hero

Harold was up at dawn. The first light, coming through thin curtains that would not meet, had awakened him, but he would have wakened in any case. Indeed, he had scarcely slept. As he dressed, with noiseless cunning, he felt stiff and chilly and knew he was catching one of his colds, but he was too excited to give it much thought.

The night before he had had to find his way by candlelight up the steep stair of the cottage where he was staying. The room had smelt musty. He suspected the bed might be damp, but he had to accept it. How like Angela not to give a thought to such a thing when arranging a room for him. Strong as a donkey herself, she treated his fear of damp as a superstition.

The three bedrooms of the cottage, one for the labourer, his wife and baby, one for Angela and one for Harold, were fitted into a space so small, the whole of it would not make a reasonable room. Angela had pointed out that a whisper in one room could be heard in all of them, so Harold must not visit her bed. Much Harold cared. His only idea had been to get off to Seaham without her and he could be sure of doing that only if he left before she woke.

He made his way down the stairs holding his breath. When he found himself outside the cottage, he felt like a volatile gas released from a bottle. With the downland turf pneumatic beneath his feet, the dew glinting in the tender sunlight, he could have sung aloud from sheer happiness. He remembered that when they were squabbling yesterday, Angela had said he only sang when he was angry. Well, he wanted to sing now, and he was not angry. Far from it. His sense of triumph over Angela proved to him she had had her day. It was all over with Angela – and for him life was taking on meaning and joy.

By some quirk of nature, Harold, a tall man with a thin, constricted look, was impelled to prefer first the company of one sex, then of the other. Although nearly thirty-five years of age, he still saw himself as a young man, one for whom life had yet to burst into the flame of its beginning. And the beginning was now. He could put everything else behind him.

For the last few months he had spent most of his time with Angela. Angela, with a responsible secretarial job in the City, had been a pleasant enough companion at first, and after repeated failure to find satisfaction elsewhere, he had even begun to think of marrying her. Heaven help him if he had! What a risk he had run! What a pass loneliness could bring a man to!

And he had been saved, only yesterday, by a remarkable thing – the most remarkable thing that had ever happened to him. A wonderful thing; a thing that had restored his faith in himself and his future, and confirmed his belief that there awaited him, that there always had awaited him, a felicity so rare that only the exceptional few ever got a glimpse of it.

Angela was spending the first fortnight of her summer holiday walking on the South Downs. Harold had agreed to join her for the week-end. When he boarded the train, he found himself alone, on a non-stop run to Worthing, with the most perfect young man imaginable. Very young, fair, athletic and . . . beautiful. Yes, beautiful; with the sort of eyes that Harold described to himself as 'my sort of eyes'. Never before had Providence done such a thing for Harold.

For the first fifteen minutes he was sick with dread of some wretched bore coming down the corridor and joining them, but no one came. As he began to relax, he wanted to speak – to reach out, to make contact, to get things started without further delay. He desired so few people that one he found so eminently desirable seemed to belong to him as by a right. But experience had taught him caution. A too impetuous approach might cause misunderstanding and spoil things before they started. He held himself in check, but he could not keep himself from looking at the young man.

Conscious of Harold's stare, the young man raised his newspaper so only his blond curls were visible above it. Harold noted the tight, shabby jeans that covered long lean legs, the old sandals that revealed the long, lean, sunburnt feet, the shirt of Madras cotton with several buttons missing. It seemed to Harold a picture of casual hard-upness, but not of poverty. It was, he decided, exactly right.

Then, suddenly, the young man lowered the paper, stared back with amused blue eyes, and *smiled*.

Harold flushed painfully. He was furious with himself but at the same time his excitement was such it almost choked him. He dared not do anything. He looked out of the window and pretended interest in the London suburbs, then in the fields and cows. He was in a stupor and it was only when he recognized the first curves of the downland that he realized how time was rushing past. If nothing happened, it would soon be too late for anything to happen. He felt panic. He searched his mind for a remark that would be an invitation but not an intrusion. He must say something that without being in any way eccentric or outrageous, would mark him as the unusual, cultivated, interesting person he was – the sort of person that must appeal to a young man like this. He turned his head but before he could speak, the young man leant forward and offered him the newspaper. In his confusion, Harold accepted it, then realized he would have to do something with it. He retired behind it. The offer might be an approach, but what a waste of time! He leafed through the pages as quickly as the situation allowed then, handing the paper back, he spoke his thanks in his high, precise voice, adding after a suitable interval: 'Lovely day.'

'Yes, splendid,' the young man agreed in what Harold was relieved to hear was 'an educated voice'. Voices did not count for much these days. Some people even admired a touch of 'regional accent', but Harold had grown up over a small grocery shop in Bradford and he frankly loathed what he called 'all that kitchen-sink stuff'. He had struggled out of it and now wanted no part of it. He often described his own voice as 'educated' and had been irritated recently when Angela had said that an elocutionist's voice was 'educated' in a sense quite different from that in which he used the word.

'Do you smoke?' the young man offered a squashed pack of cigarettes.

Harold shook his head: 'No, thank you. I have to preserve my voice.'

'Singer?'

'No. Elocutionist.'

The young man lit a cigarette then, lounging in his corner, blowing out smoke and narrowing his eyes against it, he smiled again.

Well! This was seduction if ever Harold had seen it. His frisson of response was such that he felt faint. He had never before had directed upon him such a significant and alluring smile. He glowed with gratitude. This wonderful young man was actually making the running. Had, indeed, made it from the first. He had offered Harold the paper, he had enquired if he were a singer, he had offered a cigarette . . .

Seeing himself as the pursued, Harold felt more comfortable but not a whit less excited. Here at last was the answer to all his demands on life. He smiled. At once the young man smiled again. Now Harold had no doubt about it. The situation was his.

Harold was so assured now that as the houses of Worthing appeared, he took the situation in hand: 'Would you care for a cup of tea?'

'Might as well. I've half an hour to wait for the Seaham bus.'

They exchanged names. The young man was called David. They walked down the platform together. It was only as they reached the barrier that Harold remembered calamity: Angela was waiting on the other side. How awful she looked! And she would give David a wrong impression of Harold's interests. As for Angela – Harold saw her bright, bespectacled eyes grow brighter as she saw David and noted David's good looks. Her curiosity was roused. Harold willed her to go away, anywhere, on any excuse, but of course she did not go away. As though she read his thoughts, Angela grinned at Harold, then flicked a glance at David and back again to Harold. The silly little fool, what was she trying to convey? Introduced to her, David averted his gaze and Harold could not blame him. He must have seen, as Harold himself now saw only too clearly, that she was dumpy, badly dressed and lower middle class.

Harold was on edge until he managed, behind Angela's back, to catch hold of David's hand and give it a squeeze.

[221]

David looked surprised but Harold felt sure he understood.

They went to the café beside the bus stop. Mercifully, Angela was keeping her mouth shut. She was observing them; no doubt gleefully, imagining that Harold was in for another disappointment. So long as she remained quiet, she could observe to her heart's content.

The café was hot, crowded and redolent of sweat and stale Indian tea. In precise, prim tones, Harold explained to the waitress that he wanted 'China', but either she did not know what he was talking about or pretended not to know.

David had become taciturn and Harold was certain that the presence of Angela had ruined their intimacy. He said he was 'a great walker' and asked David how far Seaham was from the village where he and Angela had their rooms. Here Angela had to chip in with the information that it was all of six miles. Did David walk much? Harold inquired. No, David preferred games and swimming. He went so far as to state that whenever he could, he spent his weekends at a Seaham bungalow.

'You stay there alone?' asked Harold.

'Usually. I'm cramming for the Oxford entrance. I hope to go up this autumn.'

'Lucky you!' For all his good will, Harold could not keep the hiss of envy out of his voice. There had never been any question of his going up to Oxford. His parents had spoiled him, they had given him every material comfort they could afford, but they would not waste money on higher education. They would not even let him try for a grant to one of the neighbouring Redbricks. They had sent him out at sixteen to serve his time in a gentleman's outfitters and he had trained as an elocutionist after working hours. He had never forgiven them. It had taken him ten years to struggle out of his class.

His father had left him three thousand pounds and, bitterly, he had seen it as the price of his youth.

David looked out of the window. His bus was about due. As he did not suggest their meeting again, Harold was forced to say: 'I was thinking of strolling over to Seaham tomorrow.'

'Some stroll!' giggled Angela.

Harold ignored her, determined not to let her ruin his last chance of arranging something with David. Desperately, he said: 'Would you like me to call on you?'

'If you like,' but David gave no information.

By questioning him, Harold learnt that the bungalow was called 'St Chad's' and was by the sea.

'Anyone'll point it out,' David said as he rose and swung a rucksack up on to his shoulder. He said 'Cheerio', giving Harold a glimpse of his seductive, significant smile, and was gone. From their first introduction, he had not looked at or spoken to Angela, a fact that Harold found satisfactory. He gazed intently from the window to watch David's light, easy jump on to the Seaham bus, and he did not return to the realities about him until the bus had driven away.

Angela said: 'What's going on? And under my very nose, what's more!'

Harold, emulating David's aloofness, smiled to himself and said: 'Never you mind.' He was determined not to tell her a thing, not a thing, and he maintained his silence as their own bus took them to Findon and they walked up to the cottage where Angela was staying. But he could not keep it up. During their afternoon walk, she made him tell her everything and by the time he had finished, she was no longer laughing at him.

'I hope you're not making a mistake,' she said.

'I'm quite sure I'm not.'

'You've been mistaken before.'

'Perhaps I have, but this was different. A special sort of understanding existing between us from the start. I felt it at once. As soon as he smiled at me, I knew. I just knew.'

'I must say, he didn't seem very forthcoming in the café.'

'That's because you were there. You don't look your best in that yellow dress. Yellow's a colour that calls for a very good skin.'

'What a waspish creature you are, Harold! – or would be if you had more energy.'

Harold felt more flattered than not by being called waspish. His face in the glass looked to him pathetic rather than dangerous, a deprived face, as though he had as a child been underfed instead of stuffed with pastries, sweet biscuits, ice-creams and all the chocolates that lost their colour when on display in the grocery-shop window. 'Cosseted and spoilt,' he thought, 'spoilt and cosseted', as though some crime had been perpetrated against him. If his mother had not kept him wrapped up in cotton-wool, he would have learnt to resist the coughs and colds that now made his life a misery. Thinking of this, he began to sing to himself in protest and Angela said: 'You always do that when you're annoyed.'

'Do what?'

'Sing to yourself.'

He was suddenly furious and he cried at her: 'You don't understand anything.'

'Poor Harold!' she sadly said.

He stopped in his tracks, turned on her and said: 'These days you are always going out of your way to annoy me. I wonder why?'

'*I* annoy *you*!' she gave an exaggerated gasp that disgusted him. Though she was getting on for thirty, she still had the silliness of the female adolescent. And God, how silly young women were! It was then that he realized that the feminine had become repulsive to him. It seemed to have happened in a moment, in the twinkling of an eye, but no doubt the change in him had been coming during these recent weeks of disagreement with Angela. It was almost impossible for him to understand how he had tolerated her for so long. Angela and he had met one wet Saturday afternoon in the Streatham public library. They had both put up their hands to take down the same copy of Maugham's *Writer's Notebook* and Harold had said impressively: 'I see we have similar tastes,' and Angela had giggled. She had then asked him what he thought of Maugham and had listened respectfully while he spoke his admiration and his reasons for it. They had walked together out of the library and after standing about talking for some time in the rain, had ended up in a teashop in Streatham Hill. He had been rather annoyed when Angela ordered a buck rarebit and relieved when she insisted on paying for it. Here was a girl whom it would be safe to see again. He found her to be no fool and not bad in bed, but what appealed to him and held him for so long was the abject humility that underlay her rather perky manner. He discovered soon enough that all the confidence had been kicked out of her by a bitch of a mother – a woman of cheap good looks, judging from the photograph that Angela kept beside her bed – who convinced Angela that she was too ugly ever to find herself a man. Angela was not ugly; just homely. She had a high-coloured bun of a face and glasses that she took off whenever possible, leaving a red rim on the bridge of her nose. She used no make-up. 'What good would it do on a face like mine?' Gradually her admiration for Harold had deteriorated, and even her sympathy had faded. When she was not treating him as a joke, she was impatient of him and was capable at times of something not far from malice.

He felt that he had borne rather a lot from Angela: he

[225]

thought of her giggle, her lack of looks and her refusal to attempt any sort of elegance. She said 'What does it matter? Nobody looks at me,' but when she was with him, people looked at the pair of them and her dowdiness was a reflection upon him. He had tried to be tolerant. Angela was his friend – for terrible moments, it seemed she was his only friend. For terrible moments he had had to be grateful to her; had had to think of marrying her. Now he was released from all obligation to her.

As she gave her vulgar, exaggerated gasp, he said: 'You know what you are – you're just an exhibitionist schoolgirl. You annoy people in order to get attention.'

That had stung her. She said: 'Indeed! Then let me tell you what I think about you. You're always saying you're an idealist – and what's the ideal? Someone who'll think you're wonderful, and who admires your voice and your piano-playing and what you call your intellect; and puts up with your self-centred conceit because they imagine you're sensitive and perceptive. Well, you may be sensitive where your own feelings are concerned, but you aren't even aware that other people have any.'

He shrugged this off: 'You don't understand. You've got no depths. You've never been clever enough – or wise enough, I ought to say – to understand how unhappy I've been. You aren't capable of understanding.'

'Everyone's unhappy.'

'Rubbish.'

'Yes, they are. Even if they don't parade their sorrows, they have them. People are full of anxiety; they don't know what hangs over them. It's not just the bomb – it's that life is so broken up and pointless. No one believes in anything, yet they want to believe. Oh, I don't know what it is, but it's the same for everyone. Your trouble is you're out of date. You want to be some sort of romantic hero lifted by your sufferings and your sensitive soul above the common run. Well, that's all over now. You've got to stop going round looking for a free gift of perfect love, and try and understand how other people feel.'

He had listened to all this very patiently in order to show her how mistaken she was. He answered seriously: 'Whatever you say, individual relationships are the most important thing in life.'

'I don't deny it. But they're not given you on a plate. You have to earn them. It's no good thinking that every pretty boy you see is going to be the great love of your life. It's jolly unlikely, apart from anything else.'

He looked at her, the poor, plain, charmless girl, and smiled: 'You know your trouble?' he said. 'You're jealous.'

'You think so? Well, it doesn't matter. The truth is, I'd be jolly glad if you did find someone who adored you. I feel sorry for you. You're so miserably lonely.'

'Don't worry about me, my dear,' he answered lightly, for he really felt now that he would never be lonely again.

As he walked towards Seaham, he could see the blue line of the sea, but it was further away than it looked. Angela had said the distance was six miles but Harold thought it must be eight or nine. He was not, as he had claimed, 'a great walker'. He occasionally took himself on solitary, reflective walks to Mitcham Common or Wimbledon or Richmond, but not much further, and there was always somewhere to stop for a cup of tea on the way. Harold would have been thankful for a cup of tea now as, sweating, exhausted and aware of his developing cold, he descended on Seaham which was not, as he had hoped, an unspoilt fishing village, but a collection of seedy bungalows and bath-huts. 'St Chad's' was one of the worst: a converted army hut. The front door stood ajar. Harold entered.

He had pictured himself arriving in time for breakfast – a late breakfast, for David would not get up very early. He might even find him still in bed and . . . but except for a couple of deck-chairs, a kitchen table, a cupboard, a sink, a camp-bed and a wireless set, the hut was empty. Harold tried to accept disappointment cheerfully. This interior was a part of David.

And David himself was not far away. He was lying on the beach, naked except for a sky-blue bathing slip, his shoulders propped against some rusty iron object left behind by the army. He had a text-book open beside him but was occupied in lazily throwing stones for a dog. As Harold's feet crunched in the shingle, he glanced round and said: 'Hallo. I'd forgotten about you.'

Even though he took this to be a coy untruth, Harold was stunned by the cruelty of such a greeting. He came to a stop and might have walked away had not David smiled and said: 'Sit down.'

Harold sat down, awkwardly, on the uncomfortable stones. Some minutes passed before he recovered his confidence and could look at David and see that he was even more handsome undressed than dressed. One direct glance at the beautifully smooth, muscled, sunburnt abdomen and chest, then David turned his gaze on the sea. He was near tears, caught between his hurt and his desire to stay until it was alleviated. For surely, if he did stay, David would make up for his brutality.

'Aren't you going to strip off?' David asked.

Harold, in an acute tone of distant refinement, said: 'I fear I have no bathing costume.'

'I've another slip on the line. Go and get it.'

'I'd rather not.'

'Oh, for Heaven's sake! You look too ridiculous here on the beach in that city gent's outfit.'

Harold forced a laugh: 'I'd look more ridiculous without it.'

'You couldn't.' David turned his back on Harold and called the dog to him. When it came, he caught it, rolled it over and pretended to wrestle with it. In the uproar that resulted, conversation was at a stop. Harold sat uneasily for a few minutes, then got to his feet and went back to the bungalow. The slip on the line was red. He took it inside the hut, undressed and put it on. He knew he was too thin and hated exposing himself. When he came out, he shivered not only from the fresh wind but from self-dislike. In the brilliant outdoor light, he felt like a shell-fish that had lost its shell. His skin was hideously white. When he appeared, walking painfully on the stones, David gave a howl of laughter then collapsed, his head buried in his arms, his whole body shaking.

Harold reproved him: 'I'm not at all well. I'm developing one of my colds.'

'Oh dear, oh dear!' David lay helplessly sobbing with laughter. When he at last managed to swallow his laughter back, he said: 'Why don't you run round a bit! It'll warm you up.'

In desolate obedience, Harold tried to run round in circles as he had seen athletes run on the screen, but the stones were agony and soon the dog, attracted by his activity, was bouncing about him, whoofing and snapping at his ankles. He found this intolerable and lost his temper in spite of himself: 'Get off, you brute,' he shouted.

It was evident that David could scarcely keep his laughter under. He called the dog and when it went to him, he cuffed it affectionately about the ears: 'I'll keep him busy,' he said and he began throwing stones again, but somehow Harold was always in the line of fire. The stones whanged round his feet and the dog, tearing after them, tripped him and sent him flying. He rose, rubbing a grazed elbow.

'Sorry!' David's shoulders were shaking again.

Very funny! Harold sat down. When the dog settled beside him, he pushed it irritably away.

'Don't you like animals?' asked David.

'They're all right in their proper place.'

'Isn't the beach a proper place? They seem right to me wherever they are.'

'Unlike human beings, you mean?'

'Well, human beings can look a bit silly at times. Aren't you going to bathe?'

'I don't think so. It's chilly. I've got a cold.'

'Then I'd get dressed if I were you. You look too awful like that.'

Harold, his eyes blurred by tears, stared out to sea for some minutes, then jumped up and returned to the bungalow and his clothing. David arrived while he was lacing up his shoes.

'How about something to eat?' David cheerfully asked.

'No, thank you. I'm going straight back.'

'Don't be an ass.' David turned on the wireless set and, without waiting to hear what noise would come from it, went to the cupboard and brought out bread, cheese, corned-beef and a teapot: 'Here!' he threw a bundle of knives and forks on the table, 'put these straight.' He lit a spirit-stove and filled the kettle.

Harold was hungry and the thought of food cheered him. He saw the hospitality as a peace offering and decided he would feel better when he had had something to eat. He would stay, but not without protest. He said in suffering tones:

'You are so different from what I imagined: so different.'

'Sorry, but it's scarcely my fault.'

Harold adjusted the wireless and found a Beethoven symphony. He stood listening, his expression becoming entranced, until David said: 'Oke. All ready.'

While they were eating, Harold did his best to cross the barrier between them.

'So you'll be up at Oxford in the autumn! I sometimes go there for weekends.'

David made no response. Harold asked: 'What do you intend to study?'

'Mathematics.'

'Good Lord!'

When the meal was over, David lit a cigarette and started clearing the table. Harold watched, making no move, while David poured water into a pan and stacked in the dishes. Throwing a damp, dirty towel towards Harold, David said: 'Let's get it over.'

Harold rose unwillingly. He hated household chores, especially dish-washing. Dish-washing was the job his mother had imposed on him at home and he had always felt it an inferior activity. With a distasteful smile on his lips he took up the towel and said: 'I'm not in the habit of washing dishes, but I don't mind obliging you,' and as he spoke, he slid an arm round David's neck. David dodged away. Without turning or pausing in his work, he calmly said: 'Pull yourself together.'

Harold stood as though he had been slapped in the face, then threw the towel aside and walked out of the bungalow. He paused in the garden, his hands in his pockets, and sang to himself.

'He's a little flirt,' he thought, 'I'll call his bluff,' but he was not certain he could call David's bluff. He went to the wooden paling round the garden and leaning over it, pressed his hands against his eyes.

David came out to hang the towel on the line. He had put on his shirt and jeans. He said: 'At four o'clock I have to go to tea with friends.'

'Don't worry, I'm just leaving.'

'No need. How about a walk along the shore?'

Harold, looking at him, met the smile again and was more disturbed than before. They went together to the water's edge and along the sand strip.

'You don't like men that way?' Harold asked after long silence.

'I find I prefer women on the whole.'

'Do you mind my being attracted to you?'

'I suppose you can't help it,' David kept bending to pick up stones and skim them across the sea, 'I'd hoped it might be possible to have a friendship without that.'

Stung to an impolitic tartness, Harold asked: 'I can't say that was the impression you gave me.'

'No? Sorry for that. I'd better be getting back. They asked me to come early.' He glanced sideways at Harold and with his provoking smile said: 'Very pretty girl where I'm going.'

'Is there?' Harold was filled with resentment. The smile now seemed unforgivable. His cold was becoming worse. The undressing had done him no good. His hands in his pockets, his eyes on the ground, he began to feel really ill.

David stopped at the gate of one of the larger brick bungalows and held out a hand: 'This is where I leave you.' Harold, ignoring the hand, brushed past him without a word. He walked with a sense of purpose until he reached the brow of the downs, then his pace slowed, weariness came down on him. For the moment he felt only anger. Misery would come later. As he trudged along it seemed to him David had encouraged him simply to make a fool of him, then, bored, had simply dismissed him. But why should he get away with it? Why should Harold let himself be dismissed like that? He was not a fool or a weakling. He came to a stop, then, obstinately resolved, he turned in his tracks and walked back to 'St Chad's'. The door still stood ajar. He went in and, wrapping himself up in a blanket from the bed, sat down beside the wireless set and found some music. The music soothed him, then a sensuous tenderness and longing began to grow in him. He became aware of mysterious desires in himself and mysterious powers. He felt he had genius of a sort, though what sort he could not tell. Intoxicated by the sense of his own personality, he was certain that when David returned everything would be different. The hours passed. He lay entranced, waiting, filled with a delicious anticipation.

The room was completely dark when David returned. He switched on the light as he entered then saw Harold and stared at him blankly. Harold gave a weak titter.

'I couldn't go all that way back. I really didn't feel well enough.'

'What's the matter with you?'

'It's this cold. It's worse. My temperature's up. I must have got a touch of chill down on the beach.'

'You'd better get into bed. I'll make you a hot drink.'

Harold took off his coat and trousers and lay on the bed in his shirt. He doubled the blanket over him. It was miserably thin. 'I'm highly susceptible to colds,' he said. Beneath him the canvas was hard and comfortless: 'I ought to have more covers.'

David took a woollen scarf from the cupboard and threw it to Harold. Wrapping it round his neck, Harold, with morose pleasure, smelt its scent of sweat and sand. He sat up in the bed, grinning wretchedly, and watched David heat in a pan some water, sugar and the end of a bottle of wine. He handed the drink to Harold by stretching from the bottom of the bed.

In silence they ate another meal of corned-beef and cheese. When it was finished and David was washing dishes again, Harold burst out: 'Why do you dislike me?'

'I don't dislike you – particularly.'

'You can't pretend that you like me: yet, at the station, you let me squeeze your hand: and you smiled at me on the train.'

'Doesn't everyone smile?'

'But not like that. You know there are smiles and smiles. You deliberately misled me.'

David went outside to hang the towel on the line.

Harold watched for him to reappear in the doorway, then accused him: 'If you didn't like me, you should have shown it straight away.'

'I suppose I made a mistake.'

'What do you mean – a mistake?' Harold sat upright in his eagerness to discuss himself. 'What is wrong with me?'

David laughed uncomfortably: 'How should I know?'

'Yesterday you were friendly. Today, straight away, you were cruel and cold. I felt you hated me. Why? For what reason? What did I do wrong? What made you change? Did you think I looked ridiculous?

'Perhaps. A bit.'

'So that was it!' Having been given the answer he expected and dreaded, Harold sank back on to the bed with quivering lips. He said: 'I've found no one to understand me . . .' there was a pause before he could control himself sufficiently to add: '. . . or accept me.'

'Sorry about that.' David lit a candle. Switching off the light that hung naked, dim and fly-blown from the centre of the ceiling, he undressed in the obscurity of the candle's light.

Watching him, Harold wondered what he would do when he was ready for bed.

To keep contact, any sort of contact, Harold asked: 'What's wrong with me?'

'How do I know? You're a bit difficult, I should say.'

'How? How am I difficult? In what way?'

'I'd call you artificial. You're not like other fellows.'

This statement of his difference filled Harold with a bleak satisfaction.

As David, in socks, pyjamas and overcoat, settled himself in one deck-chair and put his feet up on the other, Harold gave an anguished cry of disappointment. David ignored it. He blew out the candle and prepared for sleep. Harold protested out of the darkness: 'I quarrelled with my girl-friend for your sake.'

No reply came from David.

'She understands me. Why can't you understand me? She appreciates me. Why can't you? Tell me what prevents you? Tell me . . . tell me . . .'

Silence.

'I'm only down for the week-end. I've got to go back tomorrow. I've got classes in the afternoon. Poor Angela won't see anything of me. I've left her alone all day. She'll be terribly upset. She may even decide to finish with me, and then I'll have no one. I'll have no one . . . no one.'

David gave a slight snore.

Tears slid from Harold's eyes and fell to the grimy pillow. He wondered if he had spoken the truth when he said Angela understood him? Did anyone understand him? Could they understand him? At the thought of his difference, he was comforted as though he were in some way ennobled by his separation from the rest of the human race, and he at last fell asleep.

He awakened again at first light and again got himself up and dressed silently, this time in order to escape without waking David. As he walked once more on the pneumatic turf of the downs and through the gleaming dew, his spirits rose, for he was returning to Angela. Whether she understood him or not, it seemed to him then that her feminine warmth and sympathy were the most desirable things in the world.

London, 1939. Rewritten, 1964.

Innocent Pleasures

Innocent Pleasures

It was the tram-car in the Transport Museum that reconstituted Mr Limestone. Before that he had been no more than a little dust buried beneath Emily's rejected and done-for memories of Camber. She had not given him a thought for years. He was probably dead. There might be no one left in Camber who had even heard of him; yet, suddenly, there he was in her mind, as alive as he had ever been, which was not saying much.

When she went closer to read the tram-car's particulars, she was startled, for it was one of Camber's own old tram-cars. There had never been many of them and she must have ridden in this one dozens of times. It had probably taken her again and again to Mr Limestone's door and now, by some afflatus of its own, it had conjured up the man himself. It had said across the floor: 'Limestone', yet she would not have recognized it as a Camber tram-car.

Giving herself distance as though in front of a painting, she viewed the car from the front. She was struck by its elegance. With that tall, narrow prow it might have been built, like a clipper, for speed; instead, it had been a mere public conveyance, scarcely able to get under way before once more grinding to a halt.

The line had run from the north of Camber to the pier.

The tram simply went straight down and back again. She and Edward had called it 'the brown tram' to distinguish it from the green, open-topped tram that went in to the country; but now she saw it was not brown at all: it was maroon. The maroon outer casing was beautifully bright. Inside, the slatted honey-coloured seats were polished like satin, the brass-work shone. In its present shape, it was as much a museum piece as some hand-made engine of Victorian times. It certainly had not looked like this when she and Edward, a critical, impatient pair, had watched it come swinging and pinging through the dusty sunlight, or ploughing, like some lighted bathysphere, the sea-blue murk of a winter's afternoon.

Mr Limestone lived half-way between the termini. The Worples were in north Camber, which Emily condemned as 'a nothing place', and when the tram left her at Mr Limestone's door, and went on to the sea and pier and the promenade where the band played on Sundays, she wished she were going with it.

The Limestones' house, a carmine semi-detached with yellow stonework, was finer than the Worples' house, at least on the outside. It had a front garden where a wooden palette stood on an easel and told passers-by that Mr Limestone was a dentist. Because of the palette there was a general belief that Mr Limestone was 'artistic'. Nothing was said about his being a children's dentist but the patients – and these were few enough – all seemed to be children.

There was a dentist in north Camber but someone had told Mrs Worple that Mr Limestone was good with children. In those early days, when she had to accompany her children, she took the long tram journey in the belief that he, and he alone, could 'manage' them. She boasted that she could not manage them herself, a fact for which she apportioned blame equally between them and their father. Of course there had been uproar before she could persuade them to a first visit. She described the awful remorse suffered by grown-ups who neglected their teeth in childhood: 'You wouldn't like false teeth, would you?' she demanded. 'Why not?' said Edward: 'false teeth don't ache.' When nothing else would move them, she promised them two bars of chocolate apiece. As most occasions began with threats and ended with chocolate bars, the years ahead were filled with visits to Mr Limestone.

Mr Limestone had another virtue: he was cheap. It took him months, years even, to concoct his account, and then several items would be forgotten. But small though his accounts were, and overdue, they led to painful discussions about money and Mrs Worple would say that Emily and Edward did not appreciate the sacrifices that were being made for them.

'In my young day,' she said, 'children looked up to their parents. They were grateful for being alive.'

'I bet,' said Edward, bringing from Mrs Worple the bitter comment:

'Unruly children!'

This riposte, a favourite of hers, dated back to the time when a Mr Greening, a business acquaintance of Mr Worple, had called on the Worples at tea-time and been invited to join them at the table. He was a stout, pompous man who did most of the talking, and while he talked his moustache waggled in a manner that gripped the attention of the children. At first they watched, scarcely believing, then dire amusement set in. They began to laugh until, losing control, their laughter became wild. When Mrs Worple frowned at them, they exploded helplessly and rolled round and round in their chairs. It slowly came to Mr Greening that he, of all people, was the cause of this shocking exhibition. He looked at Mr Worple, but Mr Worple had a weakness. It was a serious weakness of a sort that had been unknown in fathers when Mrs Worple was young. Whenever Emily and Edward started to laugh, Mr Worple had to laugh, too.

He did his best to admonish them: 'Now, Emily,' he said, 'now, Edward.' But he was already beginning to shake and his face was red and his eyes damp with the effort to suppress his laughter.

Emily's voice rose in a shriek: 'Listen to daddy trying to talk like mummy!' and both children collapsed on the table, weeping in an anguish of mirth.

It was then that Mr Greening, observing them with disgust, said 'Unruly children!' and Mrs Worple was deeply impressed. Although he never came back to the Worples' house, she remembered him as a champion against her unsatisfactory husband and intolerable children. If he had not made his historic indictment, she might never have realized the extent of her own grievance. When things were at their worst – which usually meant, when some *jeu d'esprit* thrown off by one of them had thrown both into hysterics – she would say, as though the phrase might quell them: 'Unruly children!'

In view of this, it was all the more remarkable that Mr Limestone could manage them with nothing but his professional mystery. He did not look like a manager. Mrs Worple gave him a stare and began: 'I'm afraid you'll find them very difficult. I don't know why they behave so badly. I'm sure they couldn't have a better home . . .'

Mr Limestone murmured 'Oh, yes?' without interest, and the children felt he was on their side.

He was so small that they outgrew him in no time. He was pale, with sandy hair and a nose that looked overlarge because it was almost the whole of his face. His cheeks, brow and chin seemed to have receded, leaving the nose in possession. His shoulders, too, had shrunk so his white jackets were all too big for him and his collar always stood out at the back as though a hand had seized him by the scruff. He was gentle, but never smiled. Emily and Edward, used to their father's quick response, sometimes tried to entertain Mr Limestone but it meant nothing to him. Whether he heard them or not, he remained melancholy, perhaps intent on more serious things.

When he had to drill a tooth, he kept up a reassuring murmur of 'There, there, shan't be long now,' and at the slightest wince or whimper he withdrew the cutting point, saying: 'Easy does it. No hurry. We'll just take a little rest,' then he would go and browse among his instruments. The danger was that he might wander out of the room and not come back for half an hour or more. Once, returning and finding Emily, miserable prisoner of the chair, he said as though he had been seeking her all over the house: 'Oh, that's where you are!'

Unlike most other people in those spacious times, the Limestones did not keep a maid. The front door was opened by Mrs Limestone with her pink, empty, melted face above a long neck, a lace blouse and a lace-edged apron. She acted as assistant when her husband was forced to extract a tooth, an extreme measure that he would avoid whenever possible, and would show her strength by letting the patient grip her hand and by wordlessly guiding the movements of Mr Limestone whose fear was such he scarcely knew what he was doing.

When she was home, she kept an eye on the waiting-room and saw that no one was forgotten. When she was out, anything might happen. Once Emily had arrived for a three-o'clock appointment and getting no answer, had been about to go when the door was opened by Mr Limestone, hair towsled, eyes pink like those of a white rabbit, who hoarsely whispered 'Yes, what is it?' Then, recognizing Emily, he put her into the waiting-room where another patient, a small boy, was curled up asleep in a chair. 'Won't be a minute,' Mr Limestone said and returned to the basement. Emily waited with the sleeping boy until Mrs Limestone came back at five o'clock. 'Better go home,' Mrs Limestone said, waking the boy and packing them off as though she scarcely knew what she might find below.

Emily had spent so long in the waiting-room she could have listed every item in it. The wallpaper was aflash with shaded squares, orange, fawn and brown. A large yellowish table crowded the centre of the room. It was littered with old copies of *Little Folks* and surrounded by eight straight-backed chairs whose leatherette seats were as good as new. No one sat in them. The children always threw themselves into the broken-down, tapestry armchairs that stood, one on either side of the fireplace. Though the grate held nothing but crumpled red paper, the whole area of the fireplace was hung with brass toasting-forks, chestnut pans and ornamental bellows, and there were so many fire-irons, dogs and hobs, it was scarcely possible to fit in the little electric fire which held a bar of heat on very cold days.

On either side of the chimney-breast there were built-in cupboards which, Emily early discovered, were filled with grown-up books. It was years before she took them out and looked at them. On the shelves above the cupboards there were, besides the electro-plated toast-racks, jam dishes and other useful unused objects, statuettes of tall girls leading Alsatian dogs and small girls cuddling bunnies.

The years passed and there were changes outside in Camber, but none in the waiting-room. Even in Camber nothing changed completely. The tram-cars gave way to buses but the buses followed the arbitrary route of the tram-lines that were still there under the tarmac and could be seen in places when the tarmac rubbed away. The Band of Hope Hall opposite Mr Limestone's house was turned into a cinema, but when the Council permitted it to open on Sunday the massed Baptist choir sang outside, making so much noise that people asked for their money back.

As for Emily, waiting in the waiting-room, she had started to rummage in the fireside cupboards, hoping the hidden books would help her to solve some of life's mysteries. They did solve mysteries, but not those of this world. They all treated of one subject: Spiritualism.

At first Emily was excited by them. She had been dis-couraged by the picture of Heaven given at St Luke's, Camber (N), and had rejected it as soon as she discovered Bernard Shaw. Now she found that people called mediums were in direct touch with the Other Side and showed it to be nothing like the boring hymn-singing Heaven of St Luke's. In fact, the spirits revealed, the Other Side was much like this Side, only nicer. Innocent pleasures enjoyed here by the few, could there be enjoyed by everyone. Supposing, one writer said, you occasionally indulged in the luxury of a cigar! On the Other Side you had only to wish for a cigar and a box of the Very Best would appear in your hand.

'Chocolates, too,' Emily hoped.

The *mise en scène* where these wonders occurred was all green lawns, trees, roses, lilies, crystal fountains, sweet breezes, and balmy airs. Book after book assured the reader that the Other Side was a garden set in perpetual summer. 'It's beautiful,' the mediums said. 'Everything's beautiful.'

'And then what happens?' Emily wondered, but nothing, it seemed, happened. The Other Side was as static as the garden painted on the safety curtain at the pier concert-hall, and soon it looked to Emily just as dusty and faded.

Between visits, caught up in the rough and tumble of reality, she forgot the spirit world, but when she returned to the Limestones' waiting-room she would remember the nectar of the Hereafter and feel drawn back to it and read avidly for a while, then find it as insipid as before.

In one book a séance was described for those who, like Emily, knew nothing of procedure. When she learnt that the researchers sat round a dining-room table, she looked anew at the Limestones' table and imagined them sitting round it, fingers touching, and Mr Limestone with head raised and eyes shut, saying in his sad little voice, 'It's beautiful. Everything's beautiful.'

Emily now towered over Mr Limestone and feeling there was something ridiculous about their relationship, she resented the hours wasted in the waiting-room and said she should go to a grown-up dentist. Soon it became what Mrs Worple called 'a battle' to get her to go at all, and the battle became grim when Emily was invited to Lilac Mittens's birthday party on the same half-term afternoon that had been appointed for a session with Mr Limestone. Emily demanded that the appointment be changed. Mrs Worple refused to change it.

Though she boasted of her inability to control her children, Mrs Worple could on occasions be adamant. These occasions always related to any suggested alteration in the scheme of things. She could not bear a picture, ornament or piece of furniture to be moved from its place in the household. Arrangements made for the future must not be unmade. Appointments that had been made by letter had a rigidity all their own. Nothing would induce Mrs Worple to write to Mr Limestone and change Emily's appointment, and it was a measure of Emily's immaturity that she dared not write herself or fail to keep it. As a last resort, she burst into tears and Mrs Worple hit back by raising her eyes to heaven and asking 'Haven't I borne enough?'

When she addressed the Almighty, Mrs Worple would do so in an anguished wail that always defeated Emily. So Emily argued no more but when the afternoon came she set out early, wearing her party frock under her coat, determined to get Mr Limestone over and done with. Mrs Limestone appeared at the door with her hat on. A bad omen. Emily appealed to her in a confiding manner: 'I'm going to a party, Mrs Limestone. Do you think Mr Limestone could do my tooth straight away?'

'We'll see,' Mrs Limestone said, not committing herself, but she went straight down to the basement where Mr Limestone had his being, and a few minutes later he appeared, abject, in a newly-starched jacket, his wife at his heels, self-satisfied and a little breathless as though she had taken him by the collar and pushed him up the stairs. She now had on her rat-grey coat and imitation silver-fox fur: 'I'm off,' she said, and off she went.

Mr Limestone said resignedly, 'Come along, Emily,' and led the way to the back room where the blue plush dental chair stood in the chilly, silvery light of the half-frosted window. The upper pane that sometimes held the distraction of clouds, held nothing now but the flat, grey February sky.

Emily, sitting down, tried to hurry Mr Limestone by mentioning the party. Not listening, he said: 'Put your head back. Open your mouth. *There's* a good girl,' and went with maddening slowness from tooth to tooth. He tapped with his mirror: 'That one ought to come out.' The tooth, crowded sideways into Emily's lower jaw, had been condemned months before but Mr Limestone would never have the nerve to pull it unsupported by his wife. When Emily said nothing, he sighed and moved on to the tooth that had to be filled. Changing the mirror for a sort of button-hook, he picked for several minutes at the decay before saying sombrely: 'I'll have to cut it.'

Snatching at his natural unwillingness to act, she said: 'I could come another time.' He reflected deeply, then said:

'No. Let's get it over.'

He packed her mouth with cotton-wool, an exacting process, then brought over the drill. Knowing that any squeak or shudder would delay the operation, Emily gripped the chair-arms and watched Mr Limestone's nose that moved, too close for comfort, like a half moon across her vision. She could smell the peppermint which he sucked to sustain himself while he worked. Her fortitude was such that he said several times, 'There's a brave girl,' then: 'I think that will do. It's only a small cavity.'

The worst over, Emily relaxed, thinking that even Mr Limestone must soon be done, but it was amazing how long it took him to mix the little dab of filling. As he bent to apply it, hand trembling with creative effort, his anxiety was such that he swallowed his peppermint. He pushed and scraped at the filling, breathing loudly, taking so long that when he stepped back to survey his handiwork, Emily was ready to leap from the chair.

'We're not finished yet,' he warned her and she reluctantly put her head back on the rest and re-opened her mouth.

Mr Limestone went to his table and searched among his equipment. He came back with a sliver of whalebone which he wedged between the newly-filled tooth and its neighbour, saying: 'Don't touch that. I want the filling to dry out. It's very important it shouldn't be disturbed.'

Gagged with cotton-wool and whalebone, Emily watched Mr Limestone to see he did not leave the room. Should he try to go, she was ready, or almost ready, to jump down and seize him. Yet he got away. One moment he was replacing his instruments in their box, the next he had gone. He went so quickly, quietly and suddenly, he seemed to dissolve among the shadows at the door. She gave a cry, but too late. She listened.

Sometimes, when Mrs Limestone was home, there could be heard slight creaks and murmurs from the rooms below. Now there was no sound at all.

She felt tricked and could do nothing but wait. The waiting went on and on. There were no clocks in the waiting-room or surgery, no means of measuring time except by the change in the light. As she watched the sky turn from grey to pewter, she began to panic.

The party began at four-thirty and tea was at five. In Emily's circle it was not correct to arrive late, and one could lose by doing so. Emily had been late for the first meeting of the Drama Club and found that the elocution mistress had cast the play and left no part for her. She had never got over that and the rebuff might, for all she knew, have destroyed her chance of becoming a great actress. It was possible that Lilac's party had already begun and she sat in agony, imagining the bright room, the talk, the expectation, the brilliance of it all.

At last, unable to bear more, she sat up and considered her position. The silence was such, Mr Limestone might have sunk down into the grave; yet he must be somewhere in the house. As the shadows deepened about her, she began to imagine him down in the basement with his hands on the table, his eyes shut, his little pale face raised as he whispered to himself, 'It's beautiful. Everything's beautiful.' Fearful, she longed for Mrs Limestone to come back. 'Oh, Mrs Limestone,' she pleaded in her solitude, '*please* ask Mr Limestone to finish my tooth!' But Mrs Limestone did not come.

Growing desperate, Emily did what she had never done before: she disobeyed Mr Limestone. First she took the soaking cotton-wool out of her mouth, then she touched the whalebone filament. It was firmly fixed between the teeth and protruded so slightly, she could not get a grip on it. She might have gone, whalebone and all, but without the protecting cotton-wool, the filament cut into her lip.

She sat for some minutes on the chair edge, listening to silence, giving Mr Limestone a last chance, then she slid down and tip-toed into the hall. She leant over the basement stairs and called in a small voice, 'Mr Limestone.' There was not a breath below.

Had he abandoned her completely? Had he left the house? She descended a few steps and spoke his name more boldly. Her voice died and not a sound returned to her. She went down further, breathing the lower air redolent of cooking-fat and old floor-cloths, and saw through the shadows in the passage a daylight glimmer from a half-open door. When she paused again, she knew he was there. She could hear him breathing.

She stood, daunted by the fact he did not answer, then it occurred to her that he might be ill. He could have fainted or had a heart attack or a stroke. With this excuse for trespass, she ran on down, ready to save Mr Limestone's life. The half-open door led to the kitchen. She saw a scrubbed deal table, an old dresser, a gas-stove, a sink – but no Mr Limestone. Yet he was near. His breathing came more loudly. An inner door led to a scullery or pantry and knowing he must be there, she advanced cautiously until she could see inside. And there he was. An old dental chair, its plush bursting and spilling the interior wadding, stood inside the door and Mr Limestone was sitting in it. She edged round to view him and saw his head propped on the rest, his eyes shut, his breath puffing out between his parted lips. His expression, tranquil, almost felicitous, told her he was not ill. He must be asleep; and before going to sleep, he had pulled up the sleeve of his white jacket and thrust a hypodermic needle into his arm. His poor, thin, little arm lay on his lap with the tip of the needle still clinging to the flesh.

What an extraordinary thing to do! Having a dislike of injections herself, Emily edged nearer, repelled and bewildered, yet curious, and at her movement, Mr Limestone's eyelids fluttered. He gave her an unseeing glance then seemed to sleep again.

She said, 'I must go, Mr Limestone. I'm invited to a party,' and for the first time in their long acquaintance, Mr Limestone smiled. His smile was joyous, as though he had already reached the Other Side where pleasures were innocent and everything was beautiful.

In front of him, on a work-table, there were some small tools and a row of false teeth set in ruby gums and mounted on a base of chalk. Among the tools Emily saw a pair of pliers and stretching round Mr Limestone's chair, she picked these up and used them to pluck the whalebone cleanly from between her teeth. Her relief was such, she became flippant and said with a giggle:

'I'm sorry, Mr Limestone. I couldn't wait.'

As she spoke, the front-door banged on the floor above and the sound sobered Mr Limestone. He did not wake but his smile was gone in an instant. Emily, guilty, an intruder who must not be discovered, fled from the kitchen and made her escape through the back-garden door. Running round the side of the house, she jumped on a bus and reached Lilac's party just as the guests were going in to tea.

Imagining she would be at fault, Emily decided to tell her

mother nothing of this episode, but somehow it all came out.

Mrs Worple was surprisingly indignant: 'I sometimes thought . . . I suspected,' she said. 'Well, what a disgraceful thing!'

'What do you mean?'

Mrs Worple would say no more but when Emily next complained of Mr Limestone's slowness, her mother at once agreed it was time for both the children to attend a 'grown-up' dentist. They never saw Mr Limestone again.

He disappeared from Emily's mind and it was only now, twenty years later, that she remembered and understood Mr Limestone's blissful smile. Her mother had disapproved, yet Emily could not disapprove. His may not have been an innocent pleasure, yet it seemed to her the pleasure of the innocent.

She came to the end of the Transport Museum feeling she had had enough of the past. She had had enough of Mr Limestone, too. Faced with the Clapham traffic and the struggle to get home, she turned her back on his memory and said again: 'I must go, Mr Limestone.'

After a moment she thought to add 'Good-bye'. And that was all she could say to Mr Limestone in an age that had parted with innocence and received nothing in return.

London, 1966.